DIARY OF AN 8-BIT WARRIOR

FROM SEEDS TO SWORDS

Published in French under the title *Journal d'un Noob (Super-Guerrier) Tome II*
© 2016 by 404 éditions, an imprint of Édi8, Paris, France
Text © 2015 by Cube Kid, Illustration © 2016 by Saboten

Andrews McMeel Publishing
A division of Andrews McMeel Universal
1130 Walnut Street, Kansas City, Missouri 64106
www.andrewsmcmeel.com

18 19 20 21 22 SDB 10 9 8 7 6

ISBN: 978-1-4494-8008-0

Library of Congress Control Number: 2016934073

Made by:
Shenzhen Donnelley Printing Company Ltd.
Address and place of production:
No. 47 Wuhe Nan Road, Bantian Ind. Zone,
Shenzhen China, 518129
6th Printing — 8/27/18

DIARY OF AN 8-BIT WARRIOR

FROM SEEDS TO SWORDS

Illustrations by
Saboten

Andrews McMeel
PUBLISHING®

In memory of Lola Salines (1986-2015),
founder of 404 éditions and editor of this series,
who lost her life in the November 2015 attacks on Paris.
Thank you for believing in me.

- Cube Kid

I really ended that last entry on a cliff-hanger.

I was basically like, **"ZOMG! I heard a noise coming from my monster box! What am I going to do?!"** and then nothing.

The end.

Boom**!!!**

Just like that.

Sorry.

There was a **pretty good reason**, though. After I heard that sound, I dropped my diary and dropped my quill . . . Wait. First, let me show you the blueprints of my house.

My house plan

I made this illustration so you'll have a better idea of what happened last night. **I'm such a nice villager, huh?** Let's zoom in on my bedroom.

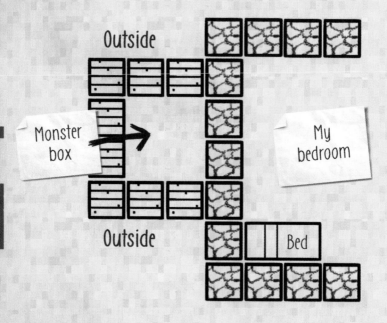

Now, I was sitting on my bed last night, and for the first time, I heard some kind of noise coming from the direction of the box.
It wasn't too loud.

It was like a little squeaking sound. At first, I just wanted the noise to go away. Then I realized . . . **it *wouldn't* go away**. Whatever it was, that mob was going to *stay* in that little room **forever and ever.**

Or at least until someone let it out. I decided that *someone* should be *Steve*. It was time to tell him about . . .

2

my plan of getting
us students
some real mobs.

I ran over to his house, but he didn't want to talk.

"I can't say anything more about those trees," he said. "Mayor's orders."

"I'm not here for that," I said. "Will you please come look at something? It's really—"

"Not tonight," he replied. "I'm starving. Not only do I have a growling stomach, but also my hunger bar is low. I'm still trying to accept this hunger bar, floating in the bottom of my vision as if it were part of a HUD in a computer game, as reality."

"You mean **people on Earth don't have hunger bars?**"

"**No,** Runt. People on Earth don't have hunger bars. They don't have anything floating in their vision. Speaking of hunger bars . . . would you like to join me for dinner?"

I glanced at the mushroom stew on his table.

"NiiuuuUUuu."

"Really? You sure?"

"NNNNNooooo. Nonono."

I ran out of Steve's house before I grew more **nauseated**. I didn't even say good-bye.

So,
Steve wouldn't be any help.

Mike was busy at his **castle-house**, working on some new lava trap he called **"The Burninator."** His face was covered in **redstone dust**.

Stump was baking with his parents. *His* face was covered with the various ingredients required to craft a cake. How that had happened, I don't know, and I didn't ask.

I could've begged **Max** for help, maybe, but . . . **no. Just no.** Someone had to open that room, all right, and

I guess that someone was going to be me.

Well, I could have asked my dad for help, but what kind of warrior would do that?

No, *I* was responsible for this. I had to deal with it on my own.

I'm brave, I told myself. Dealing with an actual mob all by myself? No problem.

It's my first quest.

But how could I talk it into cooperating? "0, hai, mob. Thanks for spawning. Can you please just be a good mob and let a bunch of villager kids beat on you with wooden swords like a training dummy? It's a good job. It pays a lot. We'll even give you healing potions to heal up all the damage so we can beat on you again."

Sigh.

Scratch that: asking nicely **wouldn't work.** I'd have to scare the mob into helping out.

I went back to my house, back to my bedroom, and made my best warrior face. When that mob finally saw me, I wanted it to know that I meant business.

I never laugh.

ALL BUSINESS. ALL THE TIME.

Now, someone looking at the above picture might think I was totally scared.

Nah.

My eyebrows were like that to help block any sunlight that might have come through the window and blinded me—**an advanced warrior technique,** see?

The sweat on my brow? I was just sweating in advance, simply **forcing my body** to cool itself for the possible heated battle ahead. My face was pale because it was trying to blend in with the cobblestone wall behind me. **That's ninja stuff right there.** As for my scrunched-up mouth, um . . . I was about to make a really scary battle cry. No scared villager here.

I walked toward the wall of my room, wielding my pickaxe.

I didn't want to mine from the outside because I didn't want anyone to see what I was up to. If anyone saw me swinging away at **my own house**, they'd certainly watch, and then they'd see whatever mob was in there, and there'd be a new **"incident."**

The funny thing was . . . my hands were shaking a lot.

I began swinging at the cobblestone wall.

Each swing seemed to take forever.

My heart was pounding in my chest. That was because I was so . . . excited? **Yes, excited.**

What kind of mob will it be? I wondered. By the sound of it, I thought it might have been a **baby ghast**. Still, I'd never seen a ghast before, only read about them. As far as I knew, they could only be found in the **Nether**. Also, there was no such thing as a baby ghast, and a normal ghast wouldn't fit in a room like that.

Hmm. It could have been a spider. It didn't sound like any spider I'd ever heard, though.

Then I thought, **maybe it's a CAVE spider?**

Wait, Mike was saying something about cave spiders. Something about how, upon seeing one, it's a good idea to run away, screaming like an enderman in an ocean biome. **Something about how cave spiders are about as dangerous as a charged creeper.** And how you should have a bucket of milk with you if you're crazy enough to face one, since milk cures poison . . . and cave spiders are

super . . .
Super . . .
Poisonous.

I immediately stopped swinging my pickaxe. Again—not that I was afraid. **Come on,** who's afraid of a little poison? Poison that makes your health bar tick all the way down until you have only half a heart left and you're so low that **even a chicken** could finish you off and the whole time you're writhing in pain, shivering? **Who's afraid of that? Not me.**

I was just thirsty. For some reason, I had a huge craving for milk right about then. I went and got a bucketful.

Actually, I came back with **two** buckets of milk. I set one down next to me on the bedroom floor. I held the second bucket in my other hand. My reasoning was: after I was done mining away at the wall of my bedroom to get to the box, I could pause real quick and drink some milk if I was still thirsty.

I began mining again.

While I mined, I held the milk bucket up **close to my lips**—how could anyone *not* want a big glug at a time like that?!

Not even afraid

Soon, the first block was mined. **I took out my sword,** but the squeaking had already stopped. **No sounds** came from within the box.

Whatever it was, it was waiting.

Hefting the pickaxe again,

I mined away the block below
and switched back to my sword.

Still nothing.

But after the second block, still nothing. **I waited:** sword ready, milk ready—nothing. Then, I ~~slowly crept toward~~ **charged into the box** and finally discovered what kind of mob was in there. **Secretly,** I had been hoping for something **epic. A poo screamer. Mungo the Overlord.** Something crazy like that.

Maybe even a **zombie cow**.
A zombie cow would have been **really cool**.

Sadly, there was no zombie cow in there.
It was . . .

. . .

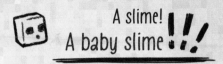

A slime!
A baby slime!!!

The smallest slime I'd ever seen. It squeaked again when it saw me. **How sad!**

Here I was, hoping it'd *at least* be a **zombie, a skeleton**, something we could practice on. I thought about smashing the slime **with my pickaxe.** That way, I wouldn't get into trouble for bringing a mob into the village, my parents wouldn't freak out, no old men would scream and get the mayor, and it'd be like nothing had ever happened. No one would know.

I could just cut my losses
right then and there. Boom.
The end of **Project Mob Spawn.**
Plus, I'd get a **slimeball** as a bonus.

I raised my pickaxe, but something **stopped** me. There was something **weird** about this slime. **It wasn't hostile.** It didn't try leaping at me. It just sat there, quivering, occasionally squeaking.

Considering that, how could I just end this creature's life?

And hey, wasn't capturing a real mob for combat class the whole reason for this in the first place?! Sure, it wasn't a zombie, but maybe this little slime had a use. We could study it, you know?

Long story short, **I have a pet now.**

11

I fed it a **piece of bread**, which it devoured in less than a second, and it became **my friend** immediately. *(Well, technically, it let out a huge belch and then became my friend, but yeah.)*

Actually, maybe I should refer to it as my "**test subject.**" That sounds way cooler than "**pet,**" right? My bedroom could become a **laboratory.** Stump could be my assistant, and we could conduct many secret experiments on this poor mob.

Can it **laugh?** Does it sleep? Will it cry if we make scary faces at it? Will it begin writing its own diary titled *Diary of a Heroic Baby Slime?*

DIARY OF A
HEROIC BABY SLIME

SLIME
SCHOOL

FOR MAXIMUM SLIMITUDE, NEVER BLOW YOUR NOSE . . . AND ALWAYS POOP YOUR DIAPER!

His future portrait

No! No! Niuuuuuuuuuuuuuu!

My pet slime **won't** be attending slime school, thank you very much. He's gonna grow up to be polite and sophisticated and an all-around good citizen. **Minecraftia's first gentleman slime.**

This will be him.

By the way, I named my pet slime Jello.

I heard Steve talking about Jell-O the other day. Apparently, it's an **Earth food** that resembles slime. I figured it'd be a good name.

Of course, I have to tell Steve about **Jello** at some point. I know that. Until then, I emptied out my double chest, and it now serves as Jello's, uh, **bed, or house, or cage,** or whatever. Jello **calmed down** a few minutes after I picked it up. Now it doesn't even mind staying in the chest with the lid closed.

Sit! Stand! Roll over! Good boy!
Now, split into a bunch of smaller slimes!

Wait. Baby slimes can't do that, <u>can they?</u>

So I have a pet baby slime, and there are more and more trees. **Yay.**

Fascinating. Yes, everyone's still freaking out and talking about them nonstop.

Steve still won't tell me what's going on.

Hmm. Actually, it is kind of weird, huh?

Why are the trees so **important?!**

Why do they matter so much?!

If anything, that forest is just **a huge source of wood** that's steadily moving closer to our village.

What's so bad about that?!

I mean, the lumberjacks in our village should rejoice. They don't even have to **move** to get their lumber anymore! They can **just sit around all day** eating pumpkin pie until the trees get close enough for them to chop.

It's like
the easiest **profession**
ever now!

In other news, a lot of people were talking at school today. Even though there's no official **ranking** of the students—as far as we know, anyway—everyone has a general idea of the **top ten** students because we're constantly peeking at other students' record books and sharing the information. Ask any student and they'll tell you:

- **Max, obviously.**
- **Yours truly.**
- **???**
- **Pebble** *(the guy Max warned me about).*
- **Donkey** *(Pebble's friend).*
- **Sap** *(another member of Pebble's crew).*
- **Stump** *(my BFF!).*
- **Porcupine** *(haven't seen him much).*
- **Sarabella** *(another member of my crew).*

- **Twinkle** *(I don't know anything about him—he's really good at crafting, supposedly).*

Now, here's where the **mystery** begins. For the past week or so, everyone had assumed Pebble was the third-highest-level student. However, someone overheard a few teachers talking after school, and one of the teachers said **Pebble** was ranked *fourth*, **not third.** But no other student has scores better than Pebble, Max, and myself. **It's weird.** Of course, there are many students out there who are **very secretive** about their scores and never give anyone the chance to peek at their record book.

I really wonder who it is? Razberry?

Nah. According to Max, he's near the bottom.

So who is this **mystery guy** with scores nearly as high as my own? And why have I never noticed him before?

As for Jello, **he's sick.** I showed my secret pet to Stump, who gave him **a slice of cake.** Jello devoured it instantly, as he does with bread, then the poor slime turned bright green and became even slimier for about an hour.

We've already learned something, then:

Slimes can't handle too much sugar.

Sticking to bread for now.

Today in school, the teachers handed out **an official textbook.** It's a new book, apparently, called the *Golden Rules Handbook.* The inside cover says:

> This collection of masterful secret tips and hints was brought to you by Urf, the masterful talented swordsman and combat guru.

Two diamond swords strapped across his back? **A bit much.** Yes, that's the guy who **almost** killed a zombie once. **With a stick.**

His handbook contains, without a doubt, **some of the noobiest information imaginable.** Still, it's required reading for all students. The elders figured it might have some stuff we missed. Here are a few of the handbook's more groan-inducing pearls of wisdom. *(Each "Golden Rule" comes with a mini fairy tale to teach us students a "valuable lesson.")*

GOLDEN RULE #1
ALWAYS BUILD A DOOR FOR YOUR HOUSE.

Once upon a time, a noob named Lenny never liked doors.

They got in his way.

They slowed him down.

He had to open them and close them.

Without a door for his dirt house, Lenny was free to run inside and outside without any delay.

Then one night, Lenny couldn't understand why so many zombies were approaching his house with their arms outstretched.

THE ZOMBIES AREN'T COMING IN FOR TEA, LENNY. OMG, THE ZOMBIES AREN'T COMING IN FOR TEA.

Seriously?
Who doesn't build doors?

It's interesting to note that this **Lenny** guy looks *exactly* like **Steve**. If you ask me, this is **Urf's** way of getting back at Steve for taking Urf's place as **combat teacher.**

GOLDEN RULE #3
MANAGE YOUR INVENTORY AT ALL TIMES.

There was once a fierce and powerful warrior named AxeNoob. Despite his name, he was not a noob but the greatest warrior in all the land. No one could chop like him. No one. But as he ventured through the land, he chopped and swung at every bush and flower he could. Eventually, his inventory, clogged with flowers, seeds, and other random items, drove this fearsome warrior insane.

THE GREATEST WARRIOR MINECRAFTIA HAD EVER KNOWN—ABLE TO CUT A SPIDER IN HALF WITH A SINGLE CHOP—AND YET, IT WAS THE FLOWERS THAT GOT HIM.

Looks like Urf tried to disguise Steve in this one. Anyway, I actually agree with the advice given. I used to gather seeds for my family, remember? Still do sometimes. After five hours of that, managing your inventory is like playing some kind of **puzzle game.**

GOLDEN RULE #5
DON'T MAKE A MUSHROOM FARM WITHOUT RECESSED TORCHES IN THE CEILING.

In a land far, far away, a noob named JonBo checked on his mushroom farm. When he opened the door, he saw not only red mushrooms growing on the floor, but also bright red glowing lights in the darkness beyond. The noob assumed those were special, glow-in-the-dark mushrooms. Overjoyed, he stepped into his mushroom farm to begin harvesting.

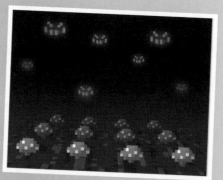

DUDE, MINECRAFTIA DOESN'T HAVE GLOW-IN-THE-DARK MUSHROOMS. THOSE ARE REDSTONE ORE VEINS, NOOB!!

GOLDEN RULE #17
DON'T MINE STONE WITH
YOUR BARE HANDS.

Long, long ago, there was a noob named Steven.

He harvested wood with his bare hands because he thought using tools was a waste of resources.

Why reduce tool durability? Why bother crafting axes at all? Steven's hands had no durability, as far as he knew. Even if it took him longer to chop down trees this way, he could save materials. He could punch and punch all day and never waste any crafting tools. Steven was the kind of guy who, after loaning his best friend a wooden sword six months earlier, would ask for exactly one stick and two oak planks to be returned.

Once, Steven and two friends bought a cake together. The cake cost six emeralds and was cut into six slices. That meant each person had to pay two emeralds. However, one of Steven's cake slices was slightly smaller than the rest, so he argued that he should have to pay only 1.75 emeralds instead.

In this one, the Steve look-alike is named "Steven." **Coincidence? I don't think so.**

At this point, the elder stopped trying to disguise his obvious jealousy:

In other words, Steven was stingy. A cheapskate. A miser. The Scrooge McDuck of Minecraftia. Minus the huge pile of gold, the black top hat, and the general appearance of a cranky, humanoid duck.

Unfortunately for Steven, he began mining stone with the same miserly logic. Why build a pickaxe? He could just mine the stone with his bare hands. And so he did.

"IT'S BEEN THIRTY MINUTES, BUT I'VE ALMOST MINED THIS STONE BLOCK! BOOM! GOT IT! WAIT, WHAT?! WHERE'S MY COBBLESTONE?!"

We get it, Urf. You're angry at Steve
for taking your job.

GOLDEN RULE #22
YOUR FISHING POLE HAS SECRET USES.

Once upon a time, in a land far, far away, oh, yes, very far indeed—approximately 18,972 blocks—Bob liked fishing.

Bob really liked fishing.

Bob really, really, really, really (really really really really really really really really really) liked fishing.

Bob was so crazy about fishing he even tried to fish in the Nether.

There were lava lakes, so why not? Maybe the Nether had some kind of fiery fish monster. Who knows? Bob sure didn't know!

Because Bob was just that crazy.
It was a
secret technique!

Bob didn't know much of anything. But he **did** know he really loved fishing. Even if he knew for a fact that there weren't any fish in those lava lakes, he'd fish in them anyway, because Bob was just that crazy.

Well, Bob fished and fished, without any luck.

He was so sad he tried reeling in a ghast just so he could say he caught something.

IT SEEMED LIKE A GOOD IDEA. ONCE HE REELED IN THE GHAST, HE COULD CHOP IT WITH HIS SWORD.

Right. A secret technique. When the ghast was only two blocks away, it spit a fireball at Bob that Bob couldn't dodge. Bob made farting/gurgling sounds as he melted into goo.

THE END.

Seriously,
this is the level of advice
Urf's book contains.

Golden Rule #31 was **the worst,** though.

GOLDEN RULE #31
LILY PAD

There wasn't a fairy tale with this one. No text at all, in fact. <u>Just a picture of a lily pad.</u>

I'm . . . not sure what to make of it.

Today wasn't all bad, though. In combat class, **Steve** showed us how to never fall off a ladder. He said it's possible to dig straight down using this method. You'll never fall off. All you have to do **is crouch while holding onto the ladder.**

Actually, Steve didn't appear to be holding on to ANYTHING. The guy's a master.

Today was bad.
Really bad.

After Crafting Basics, I saw **Pebble and Max** talking in the hall. At some point, Pebble took Max's record book, **tore** it into pieces, and threw the pieces **on the ground.**

"I thought you were the **top student**," Pebble said to Max, "the best of the best. What happened there, **ace?**"

Pebble's friends **Sap and Donkey stepped** on the fragments of Max's record books.

27

All three of them are high-level students, **just under Max and me.** They're all very skilled in combat and mining.

Strangely, Max didn't respond.

He simply stood there, **seemingly calm.**

"Aren't you gonna say something?" asked Pebble.

Donkey snickered.

"Too bad about your record book. Maybe you can tell a story about it."

I watched the whole thing in disbelief. For the longest time, I had considered Max a bully—but these guys were, like, **super bullies.**

I hadn't even noticed them before, but now they were acting like total punks.

It's just like Max said. They know graduation is coming soon **and want to finish in the top five.** The competition this year is getting **really insane . . .**

Pebble rammed his shoulder into Max and said something. He kept his voice low. I had to strain to hear it:

"Better not participate in the next mining test, ace," Pebble said. "Wouldn't want you to get **hurt.**"

Max still said nothing, looking down at the pieces of his record book. **I had to step up and say something.**

I walked up next to Max and nudged him with my elbow. "You know, the elders said the rising ocean levels were due to the melting ice plains biomes. But as it turns out, it was because of Pebble's river of tears after he **bombed** the last test."

Pebble's face momentarily resembled **a creeper's.**

Yeah. Saying that was a bad idea.

"Well, look at that," he said. "Just who I wanted to see next!"

Sap and Donkey sprinted over to me, lifted me up by the robes, and took **my record book out.**

Pebble grabbed it and **tore it into tiny little pieces.**

It happened so fast!

It was as if part of my **body had been torn up.** I'll admit **I nearly cried** staring down at my shattered record book. All that hard work . . . Gone. *(At least, until I coughed up the emeralds for a new one. Those punks.)*

The three **laughed** and walked off.

* * *

I glanced down at the **purple fragments.**

The pieces crumbled into bright violet dust—the magical energy of the book's enchantment. The dust soon faded away . . .

I approached Max. He was picking up the pieces of his own book. Not that it mattered. **The book was no longer functioning.**

"So you were telling the truth," I said. "Those guys really have it out for us."

"Yeah. Told you this is bad."

"So, what are you gonna do?" I asked.

"Nothing."

"What about our record books? We can get new ones. Let's go to the **head teacher** and pay up. Tomorrow, **we'll flash them in Pebble's face** and thank him for making us get new, shiny record books. And then we can argue with each other about how low our scores are."

Max shook his head. "Didn't you hear? They raised the price on them. They're **fifty emeralds** now. Why do you think those guys did that?"

What?!

Fifty emeralds?!
Wow, I thought, this is bad.
Where am I gonna get fifty emeralds?

"What about your parents?" I asked. "I thought your family was **wealthy.** Say, can I . . . **get a loan?**"

"Sorry, Runt, but after the pickaxe incident, **they cut me off. I'm broke. They aren't even giving me lunch emeralds. Razberry's been sharing his with me.**"

"**We've gotta get back at them,**" I said.

"No, I think I'm out." Max slipped the pieces of his record book into a pocket of his robe.

"I'm just gonna tread water from now on. After all, I wanted to be a librarian, remember? Striving to be a warrior . . . **honestly,** it's not worth dying over. Didn't you hear what he said about the mining test? Pebble's father is gonna rig the test somehow."

"How would his father manage to rig the test like that, though?"

Max gave me that cold look again.

"**You really don't get it, buddy boy.** Pebble's family goes way back. They've got connections. **His father is best friends with the mayor and most of the elders.** He's also the **head miner.** So, when the school holds that mining test, who do you think the teachers are going to ask for advice?"

"Pebble's father."

"**Right.** He'll probably suggest an area with a lot of sand and gravel. **A dangerous area.** An area he knows. And he'll fill Pebble in on where to go."

I recalled what Max had said earlier . . . Something about **a cave-in.**

Gravel or sand from up above could come

down and **crush someone** . . . **Hurrrrrrg.**

Things were getting **so serious.**

Bullies tearing up record books.

Powerful families **pulling strings** behind the scenes.

The mayor and the elders, who won't tell us anything about the trees.

The mobs, who never came back after Steve and Mike kicked their

behinds. Suddenly, **I opened my mouth** . . . and said something I

never thought I'd say.

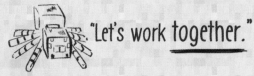 **"Let's work together."**

It seemed my words **shocked** Max as much as they did me.

He lowered his glasses.

"W-what did you say?!"

"You might've **pulled a lot of pranks on me**," I said, "but those

guys . . . if they become warriors, I'll never feel safe. In some ways,

they're worse than the mobs! Anyway, it's just like you said. If

they're out to get us, then we've gotta stick together."

"You sure about this?"

"**Yeah.** But if you pull any tricks, Stump and I are gonna harass

you until you're rank 150. **Got it?**"

"Don't worry about that," he said. "No tricks. I promise."

He paused, as if thinking about something, then said,

"I have an idea."

"What idea, hurrrrr?"

"I need some time. I'm still not sure how well it'll work. Over the weekend, gather as much sand as you can. We'll discuss it next Friday."

"Sand?"

"Just trust me."

Hmm.

Trusting Max . . . It seems difficult.

But I suppose I need him.

And then, he needs me, too.

I needed to clear my head after yesterday. So this morning, I took off for the park. **Alone. Yes, our village has a park.** It's pretty much like a forest near the middle of our village. People go there to relax, but **it's actually a tree farm so we can harvest wood safely** without ever stepping outside the walls. There are also lots of flowers for dyes.

An outsider noob came out here long ago, wanting to dye his armor red. But I guess this world is different from the game he used to play . . . **because his armor turned pink** instead.

"Don't worry, bro. You look cool. You look cool."

So there I was deep inside the park, enjoying the **beautiful scenery.**

At one point, I had the urge to check my record book—an instinct by now—but it wasn't there. **Fifty emeralds . . .** Would I ever be able to earn that many? Maybe I could **sell Jello** to some old rich guy who likes exotic pets . . . Then I had a weird feeling—you know, that creepy feeling, like you're being watched? **Yeah. That one.**

Moments later, I caught sight of something out of the corner of my eye. Like a shadow. **So weird.**

It vanished as quickly as it had appeared.

Of course, I immediately thought of the "**Village Creeper**" that supposedly sneaks around in our village. **Great.** Things sure were getting better. Yesterday, **I was mugged by a bunch of punks.** Today, I was all alone in the park, with a creeper hunting me.

Not good!!!

I heard the rustle of grass behind me. **I whirled around . . .** but there was nothing. Just the beautiful, flowery forest.

Was I seeing things? **Hearing things?** Maybe I was too stressed out. I shook my head, rubbed my eyes. And when I reopened them . . . **a girl was standing before me.**

35

I knew her. **Breeze.** She was a student. I'd seen her from time to time, although we didn't have many of the same classes and she usually kept to herself. She was pretty **shy.** Even so, she was one of those students who asked me questions after I aced a building or trading test. She **smiled.** I couldn't return the expression. Not today. What did she want, anyway? Why was she following me?

Honestly, it was a little creepy.

"I haven't seen you in a few days," she said. "What have you been up to?"

Um . . . yeah. She was acting like we were **old friends** or something.

"I'm **busy**," I said.

"You always say that," she said, her voice cool. "Anyway, you don't seem busy. Let's hang out."

"No, thanks."

Her smile faded. "What happened?

You seem so upset."

There was no way I was going to tell her about yesterday. I'd only talked to her a few times before, and it was mostly just stuff like,

"I can't teach you; uh, I'm sick tomorrow."

Then again, from what I know, she comes from a **wealthy family**, like Max.

Her parents are miners. Supposedly, they once **found a cave loaded with diamonds.**

I could have asked her for a loan, perhaps, but . . . **no.** I didn't want to be in debt to a stranger.

"I just wanna be left alone," I said. **"Okay? Is that possible?"**

She nodded and **zoomed off into the trees.** She ran so fast. In her black outfit, she looked like a blurred shadow. I thought I saw tears in the corners of her eyes. Or did I imagine that? What's with that strange girl? I thought. Come to think of it, I've seen her a lot recently. At the blacksmith. Near the well. In the hallways at school. But always from a distance. **Watching me. Seriously weird.** Why was she following me like that?

Whatever.
I whipped out my shovel and within
thirty minutes had gathered half a stack of sand.

I had my Sunday all **planned out.**

Step 1: Feed the slime.

Step 2: Go bug Steve and Mike on their day off!

I tossed Jello a bread loaf, grabbed my shovel, and ran out the door. *(Hopefully, my parents wouldn't discover my new pet.)*

Within minutes, I was at **Steve's** house. He and Mike were both there. Mike was seated at the table, **looking a little angry,** or at **least not happy.**

Steve was hunched over a furnace, his face blank, as if he was thinking very hard about something.

I decided to break the silence with a friendly greeting:

"Hey, guys. **How's the forest?**"

Before, villagers often asked something like "How's the weather?" but lately it's **"How's the forest?"** Meaning that **weird** forest in the east. Now, I didn't ask this to try to get Mike and Steve to tell me about their secret. It was just a greeting, **I swear!** But the two outsiders **glared at me.**

"We still can't tell you anything," Mike said. "So stop asking, buddy boy."

"That's fine," I said. "I have **a secret of my own.**"

Steve looked up from the furnace.

"What secret?"

"**Ohhhhhhh nothing.** But I bet it's more interesting than a bunch of trees."

Mike smirked.

"You'd be surprised."

Suddenly, Steve **pounded** the furnace with his fist.

"I can't stop thinking about **pizza! Pepperoni. Cheese.** Oh, I'd give anything for some black **olives!**"

"I'm not a fan of olives, myself," said Mike.

I stared at both of them.

"What are you guys talking about, **hurrrr?**"

Mike gave me a pitying look, as if I wouldn't understand a thing, even if he explained. Steve ignored me. **There was a feverish gleam in his eyes.**

"Those mobs, they're so **smart,**" he said. "This is how they get you . . . they made us afraid . . . holed us up in this village . . . limited our food supply . . ."

There was an **awkward silence,** then Steve spoke up again.

"Every day it's bread, bread, bread . . . and if you're lucky, steak and potatoes. **I'm sick of it!**"

"I'm sick of you talking about it," Mike said.

Steve stepped over to the crafting table. A huge amount of food items had been piled onto that massive chunk of wood.

"Pizza," he said. "What about pizza? Is it possible? Maybe if we just arrange these bread loaves like so . . ."

Mike rolled his eyes.

"Dude. No tomatoes. No tomato sauce."

"Burritos?"

"No flour. No tortillas."

As they talked—naming an exhaustive list of foods I'd never heard of—I said nothing, totally confused.

"How about an omelet?" Steve asked. "We've got eggs! We've got mushrooms!"

Mike closed his eyes this time.

"Again, I've already tried that, man. Every possible configuration. Eggs with more eggs. Eggs with milk. Eggs with mushrooms. Even eggs with a potato."

Steve gasped. "Omelets with diced potato chunks?! Who does that?! Wait, what am I saying?! I'd settle for that!"

"You're really freaking out, dude. Chill."

"How about cheese?"

"Nope."

"Butter?"

"Went through five buckets of milk trying to figure that one out."

The desperation in Steve's voice was heavy as he said,
"Apple . . . pie?"

Mike shrugged. "It should be possible, considering the fact that this world has apples, pumpkins, and pumpkin pie. However . . ."

"No apple pie?! And we can't even have toast! **Not even dry toast without any butter!** We have loaves of bread, right? But the furnaces won't toast the bread, and swords won't cut the loaves! No matter how many times I try, the bread just **<u>crumbles!</u>**"

More silence.
Mike and I exchanged **worried glances.**

Steve **scratched** his chin.

"And yet, they have **ice cream**, these villagers. Many flavors, too. But not the ones I like! **What kind of world is this?!**"

Mike rose up from his chair and looked out the window.

"A Minecraft world."

"You know, I've been thinking about quitting," Steve said. "Quitting teaching and building a **redstone robot**."

"And what would the purpose of this . . . **redstone robot** be, Steve?"

"A food-crafting robot. **Night and day**, it'd set random types of food on the crafting table, until it finally found a new recipe."

41

"That's the **most ridiculous** thing I've ever heard you say," Mike said, turning back to the window. "Not even **Marky** could build something like that! **And the guy's a crafting master!**"

Steve's eyes lit up.

"Marky! Yes! If only **Marky** was here! He'd know **how to craft pizza!**"

"But he's not here, Steve. Accept it. Until we figure out a way to get back to **Earth**, it's potatoes and bread."

"I'll teach a golem to craft food for me!"

"No, you won't."

"Yes, I will! It will craft while I sleep!"

Mike groaned, but Steve just laughed.

"Supreme pizza, **here I come!!**"

Yeah.

Needless to say, I didn't hang around there much longer. I understood what was going on, though. Steve missed **Earth food**, stuff like **pizza** and **hamburgers**, things I've never eaten before. **I guess they must taste amazing.**

Still, I don't get it—what's wrong with our ice cream? Maybe he tried that **nasty Creeper Crunch?**

 It is really
gross.

Later, I went back to the park with Stump. That's where the ice cream
shop is.

While Stump and I got ice cream,
I felt like someone was watching me again.
I didn't see anyone, though.

Dear Diary,

I like you, diary, I really do. But I can only assume you're going to suffer the same fate as my **record book.** Torn to pieces, crumbling into nothingness. You see, Pebble and his friends shook me down today. Took everything I had, from my **sword** to my **lunch emeralds**. Well, **almost everything.** Thankfully, **Urf** arrived just before they grabbed you, diary. But it's only a matter of time.

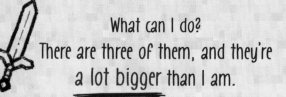

What can I do?
There are three of them, and they're
a lot bigger than I am.

Stump tried to **help out**. I warned him not to. He's probably next on their list. Even though Stump is the **seventh-highest-level student,** he's still a threat.

Worse yet, that Porcupine guy has apparently joined Pebble's crew. Porcupine saw Pebble pushing me around and figured he'd be better off with **the punks.**

So all the top students . . . they're taking sides. You're either on **my crew** or on **Pebble's** . . . and it's easy to see which crew is the strongest.

I saw **Sarabella** hanging out with **Donkey.** She gave me a **guilty** look.

"I'm sorry," she said later. "It's just . . . if I keep talking to you, they'll **harass** me, too, you know? I just wanna graduate with good scores."

I looked away.

"Yeah. **It's fine.**"

"We're still friends, right?"

"Sure."

I totally understand, though. I'm not bitter.
<u>Team Runt</u> is a sinking ship.

Didn't bring the diary to school today. **Didn't bring anything.** Except a **carrot.** My lunch.

A single carrot. Not two carrots, not a carrot and an apple. A single carrot. THAT'S POOR, OKAY?!

So go ahead. Beat me up. Take everything in my inventory. **Well, today,** Team Pebble tried just that.

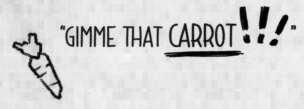

"GIMME THAT CARROT!!!"

But when they grabbed me, I immediately whipped out my carrot and ate it as fast as I could. They struggled to take **my only food item** away from me. I chomped down faster. Little pieces of carrot went flying everywhere.

OM-NOM-NOM-**NOM**-NOM.

"Get that carrot!"
"Grab it!"
But I managed to eat it before they took it from me.
"You little noob!" shouted Pebble.
Even as they roughed me up, **I smiled.**
It was a **small little victory** today. They couldn't do anything to me. The only item they could have taken I ate right in front of them.

Good game. Noobs.

OOF !
OOF !

Those sounds came from me. Team Pebble walked up and said they weren't going to steal anything today; they were going to *give* me something. They gave me a **pumpkin**, all right—jammed it down over my head and began punching me. "Don't just stand there!! **You're a pumpkin zombie, little noob!!** It's combat training!!"

OOF!!
OOF!!
OOF!!

I don't want to write much today.

I . . . will . . . get . . . my . . . **revenge.**

But I can't feel sorry for myself. The things they did to Max were even worse.

**Really wish he'd hurry up
with that big idea of his.**

"You like eating things, **do you?!** Let's see if
you can eat this **whole cake!!**"

That about describes my day. By the way, that wasn't their cake.
It was Stump's. Something he'd made in Crafting Basics.

Max.
Please.
Hurry. Up.

Pebble **didn't try** anything today. It's because a new **rumor** has been spreading through the school—in fact, spreading through the **entire village**. Supposedly, someone spotted **an enderman** in the village. A friendly enderman who only wanted to **trade.** He was looking for a potion. And not just any potion, but a **Potion of Water Resistance.** This isn't something that prevents drowning damage but . . . damage from water. I've never heard of such a potion, and neither has anyone I've talked to. Yet . . . that doesn't mean such a potion doesn't exist.

Now, here's the thing.

The enderman is willing to pay **five hundred emeralds** for a stack of such potions. **Five hundred emeralds.** This enderman is rich, apparently. **Of course,** everyone in the village started freaking out. Especially the kids at school.

"We've **gotta find out** how to craft that potion!!"

"We've gotta make some before that enderman returns to the village!!"

"With that many emeralds, I can buy an **enchanted diamond sword!!**"

Like that. Forget the **trees**—the enderman was all anyone was talking about. As the rumor goes, the enderman is a world traveler and has a dream of becoming a **professional swimmer. The problem** with that, obviously, is that water is like **acid** to endermen. They can't even be out in the rain, much less swim for any length of time. But this Potion of Water Resistance would fix that, **I guess.**

"Finally! My dream will come true!!"
GLUGGLUG
GLUGGLUGGLUG.

The rumors were flying even more today.

People kept talking about what they were going to do with their massive pile of emeralds once they discovered how to brew that potion. That girl **Breeze** came up and asked me about it. She keeps talking to me every chance she gets. **What is her problem?!**

Later, I ran into Max. He apologized for being late. While we stood there in the streets, we heard kids nearby talking about the enderman. Max gave me **an evil grin.**

Suddenly, **I understood—he** was the one responsible for those rumors. That meant the rumors weren't true. The enderman didn't actually exist. The world-traveling enderman was just another one of **Max's creations,**

like the poo screamer.

Yes, Max was at it again with his crazy tales—and this time, I didn't mind them at all. It's like this: Everyone's gonna be crafting potions for at least the next few days, experimenting, trying to figure out how to make that special potion. And what do you need when crafting a bunch of potions? **Empty glass bottles.**

"Supply and demand, buddy boy. Supply and demand."

Max went around the village and **dug up every sandy area** he could. I dug up a bunch myself in the park. We figure we probably have at least **75% of the village's available sand.** At least, the easy-to-find stuff.

When people run out of bottles, they'll have no option but to come crawling to us. **We'll be able to charge anything we want for them.**

I have to admit, this plan of
Max's is pretty brilliant.

This morning, I finished reading Urf's *Golden Rules Handbook*. At the end, there was an advertisement for his next book . . .

The Ultimate Legendary Handbook.

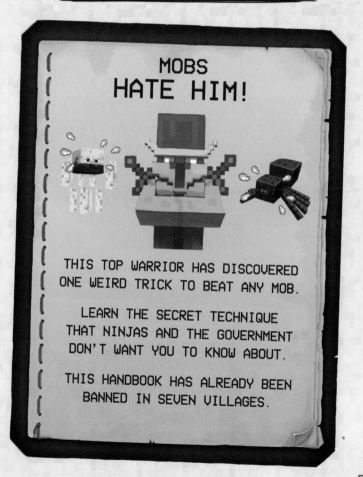

MOBS
HATE HIM!

THIS TOP WARRIOR HAS DISCOVERED
ONE WEIRD TRICK TO BEAT ANY MOB.

LEARN THE SECRET TECHNIQUE
THAT NINJAS AND THE GOVERNMENT
DON'T WANT YOU TO KNOW ABOUT.

THIS HANDBOOK HAS ALREADY BEEN
BANNED IN SEVEN VILLAGES.

55

"BEING A SKELETON USED TO BE SO EASY . . . UNTIL THE ULTIMATE LEGENDARY HANDBOOK CAME OUT. FOR ALL THE MOBS OUT THERE, IF YOU RUN INTO A NOOB--AND HE'S CARRYING A COPY OF THE HANDBOOK --WELL, JUST RUN. JUST RUN."

—SKELLA BONINGTON

TIRED OF BEING A NOOB?
DO YOU WANT TO BE A PRO?
READ ON FOR A SAMPLE OF *THE ULTIMATE LEGENDARY HANDBOOK,* WRITTEN BY URF.

ULTIMATE LEGENDARY SECRET #1:
USE A SWORD TO ATTACK MOBS.

Once upon a time, a noob named Mike was a total noob. He was almost as noob as Steve the Noob, who was the mayor of Noobtown. Mike was so noob that he didn't use a sword. He thought using a stick as a weapon would be almost as good.

"HMM. I GUESS THIS SWORD COULD USE SOME ENCHANTING."

ULTIMATE LEGENDARY SECRET #2:

EVEN MUNGO IS AFRAID OF *THE ULTIMATE LEGENDARY HANDBOOK.*

"MUNGO SCARED.

URF BOOK MAKE TINY MAN TOO STRONG.

SO, MUNGO BECOME FARM MAN.

MUNGO SAD NOW.

MUNGO NO LIKE FARM WORK.

MUNGO NO LIKE EAT ORANGE THINGS.

AND BROWN THINGS NO TASTE GOOD!!

BUT EASIER THAN EAT TINY MAN. URF

BOOK MAKE TINY MAN TOO SMART.

OK, BYE. MUNGO GO EAT PIE-PIE NOW."

ULTIMATE LEGENDARY SECRET #3:
URF IS WAY COOLER THAN STEVE.

"I used to be a bad warrior . . . For example, I once hugged a creeper because it looked sad and I thought it needed a hug.

"But not any longer. After reading *The Ultimate Legendary Handbook*, I'm now a combat teacher.

"Urf taught me everything I know and I'm so thankful for that.

"Someday, I hope to be as amazing as Urf. It's not possible, but I still try."

—STEVE

Ahem. Runt here.

My first thought upon reading this advertisement was:

What?! Steve wouldn't say something like that! **Urf clearly made that up!**

Hurrrr. Urf better be careful. When Steve finds out about this—and he will—he's gonna **explode** like a **mountain made of TNT**—and not just *any* mountain made of TNT, but one inhabited **by creepers.**

Boom Mountain. It makes the Nether look like a Flower Forest.

Anyway, what am I doing thinking about **Urf** and **Boom Mountain**?! Today was a **big day!** Max came up with a **clever plan** to earn the emeralds we need to buy new record books. It was pretty simple.

1) Max cooked up a story about an **enderman** who wants to be a professional swimmer and is willing to pay **five hundred emeralds** for a Potion of Water Resistance *(so he doesn't burn while in the water).*

2) After hearing about the enderman, kids at school **freaked out.** They wanted to **brew that potion.** Kids kept bugging the brewing teacher about it. *"How do I craft one?" "What's the secret recipe?"* And so on.

3) Max and I dug up **most of the sand** around the village. *(You need sand to make glass, glass to craft bottles, and bottles to brew potions.)*

4) Yesterday, we spent hours **crafting bottles** and set up a stand to sell them:

BOTTLES
SEVEN EMERALDS
PER STACK

Stump wasn't interested in selling bottles, but he brought a **bunch of cakes**. He didn't sell many . . . and I'm *so glad he didn't.*

Because an hour after we set up our stand, we were so **swamped** with customers there was no way we could take a **lunch break**.

Stump's cakes were the only food we had. *(Even if we had remembered to bring lunches, our inventories were too clogged with bottles.)*

Within an hour, we made **twenty-one emeralds!** A bunch of other kids just stood around, though, asking us to lower our price.

What can I say?
Villagers will be villagers.

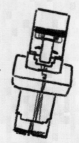

I had that creepy feeling that someone was **watching me** again. Which was **strange**, because obviously, a lot of people were watching me. I wonder why I had that feeling?

Anyway, it seemed we were going to make the **hundred emeralds** we needed. Sadly, things never come easy for me, and today was no exception.

There was a **shout** nearby.

You've got to be kidding me . . .

It was Pebble. "**Finest-quality** bottles!" he called out. "Only **six emeralds** per stack! Get 'em while ya can, folks!"

People rushed over to his little stand—a flood of **cries, shouts,** and **elbows.** Through the crowd, I saw Pebble give me a wink.

Urg!!!

What a copycat. His bottle stand was like a smaller version of ours. All he did was copy us . . . and offer a **slightly lower price.**

What a poo screamer. I put up a new sign:

BOTTLES
FIVE EMERALDS
PER STACK

Boom !!!

That'll fix him, I thought.

In response, Pebble dropped his price to **four.**

BOTTLES
FOUR EMERALDS
PER STACK

So, we went to **three**.

Then *he* went to **two** . . .

It was a price war—**Bottle Mart versus Dork Depot**. Finally, I dropped our price to **one emerald per stack**. There was no way he could go any lower, right? He'd have to match our price, and we'd get half the customers. **Right?**

I . . . **couldn't believe** what that punk did next.

Free?!
Seriously?!

I'm gonna **hurgg,** I thought.

Yeah. I can definitely feel **a big one coming on.**

Okay.
Calm down.
Calm down.

I stood there until I no longer had the urge to **hurgg.**
Then an idea suddenly hit me, like lightning **hitting**
a pig and turning it into a **zombie pigman.** Except,
uh . . . I'm not a zombie pigman. I'm not a pig, either.

Gah. Never mind.

Anyway . . . **My idea was this:** I had managed to peek at
Pebble's record book earlier. By doing that, **I learned his weakness.**
You see, his crafting score is his lowest score. Brewing is a subskill of
crafting, which means he doesn't know how to brew very well.

Why does that matter?

It will become clear **soon enough.**

I turned to my friends: "Max, go to school and grab a brewing stand.
Stump, go to my room and grab **two nether warts, two rabbit's
feet,** and **a water bucket. Oh,** and a pinch of glowstone dust."

Looking at their faces, you would have thought I'd just
invited them to a slumber party in the Nether or something.

"Huh?! Why?!"

"Because it's time to **humiliate** our competition," I said. "And don't
forget the glowstone!!"

Away they went. **I left our bottle stand** and walked into the crowd.

"Everyone, if I may have your attention," I called out. "It seems there's
only one way to determine who has the highest-quality bottles:

a brew-off!!!"

People turned to me with confused looks.

"A brew-off?"

"Hurrr? What's that?"

"It's like a dance-off," I said, "except with brewing, not dancing. A competition." The crowd broke into low murmurs. Hushed excitement. Laughter. Even a few cheers.

Pebble scowled and pushed through the crowd. "So, it's a brew-off you want, eh, buddy boy?! You don't have a brewing stand!"

Then someone cleared his throat. "Ahem." Max was standing behind Pebble, brewing stand in hand. He must have sprinted the whole way. He set it down between Pebble and me.

I smirked. "You were saying?"

Beads of sweat formed across Pebble's brow.

"Err . . . ahh . . . well, y-you need more than just a brewing stand! You need ingredients too! Wanna brew Air Potions, do ya?"

Grrrrrrr. He can laugh all he wants, I thought, but if my idea works, he's gonna be the laughingstock of the whole school.

Thankfully, Stump showed up moments later with all the ingredients and a water bucket in hand. "Here you go, cap'n."

"Looks like we have everything we need," I said, looking Pebble in the eye.

Pebble swallowed nervously and wiped his brow.

"W-well, yes," he said, "but I w-wouldn't wanna **embarrass** you in front of a-all these kids! You sure you want that?"

"Oh, I'm sure," I said, with a nod.

I gave Pebble one nether wart and one rabbit's foot. Then Stump **dug a hole** and emptied the bucket into it.

From left to right:
Stump, Runt, Max, and Pebble.
Hurrm. Again,
it felt like someone was
watching me . . .

I addressed the crowd.
"The brew-off has officially begun!"

Everyone backed up to watch the show. The chatter grew louder.
I raised **an empty bottle.**

"We will test the quality of our bottles by brewing Potions of Leaping," I said. "We'll then **drink our potions,** and the one who **jumps the highest . . ."**

Of course, even if the glass I'd used had somehow been of higher quality, it wouldn't have affected the potion at all. You needed **extra ingredients** for that, like **redstone or glowstone dust.**

I was just **bluffing.**

A lot of the people in the crowd didn't seem to catch on to this. Probably most of them hadn't paid too much attention in brewing class. Or perhaps they questioned it but weren't sure enough to say anything. After all, Stump was nearby, and his crafting score was **really high.**

Pebble stepped up to the brewing stand.

"I'll show you how it's done, kid."

He whipped out one of his bottles, filled it with water, brewed an Awkward Potion with nether wart, and finally, a **Potion of Leaping** using a **rabbit's foot.**

Ta-daaa

The brewing stand bubbled away.
After Pebble's potion finished brewing,
he held it up **triumphantly.**

There were a few **cheers**—and gasps—from some of the younger
kids. It might have been the **first time** they'd ever seen a potion.

"Wow!"

"**Cool!**"

"It's so shiny!"

I nudged Stump.

"Hey!" I whispered. "**Dust me!**"

"Oh. Right."

Stump slipped me some **glowstone** dust. Luckily, Pebble kept
showing off his potion to the crowd.

"**See that?** The **best** bottles in the village! Forget those **noobs!**
Use my bottles or don't brew anything!!"

All eyes were on him at that point, which allowed me to add some glowstone to my Potion of Leaping without anyone noticing.

Within ten or so seconds, I brewed . . .

. . . a Potion of Leaping II:

for when you absolutely, positively need to **bounce around** like a slime.

This would allow me to jump higher than Pebble, since he'd only brewed **a standard Potion of Leaping.**

Yeah, **I cheated.**

But you know what? **That guy deserved it.** Besides, when the mobs come knocking on our iron doors again, I highly doubt they're going to **play fair . . .**

As soon as I brewed my potion, the crowd grew noisier. **They wanted us to chug.** Pebble slammed down his potion, then tossed the bottle aside and glared at me.

"Bottoms up, **noob.**"

I did the same. Immediately after, I felt **sick,** as if I'd eaten too much ice cream or something.

Pebble jumped up into the air. He jumped maybe **half a block** higher than normal, landed, and jumped again.

"What's up, kid?!"

I grinned and said, "About to set **a new record,** that's what's up."

70

"Yeah, yeah. Let's see it."

"On three," I said. "One, two, thr— eeeeeEEEEEEEEEEEEEEEEEEEEEEEE
EEEeeeeeeeeee . . ." (As I jumped, the word "three" turned into a thin, catlike scream.)

You see, I jumped kinda high. Like, **really high** . . . Honestly, there were better words than "jump" to describe what I was doing, really. Like "fly."

I'll admit it—**I was terrified.** Terrified and **confused.**

Why did I leap so high?
A Potion of Leaping II should have made me jump one and a half blocks higher . . . **not one hundred.**

"STUMP!!
I SAID A PINCH OF
GLOWSTONE!! A PINCH!!"

That was when I saw it. The forest.

Of course, **it had grown** over the past few days. From up here, I could see how **massive** it really was. Dark oak trees, tall and thick, stretching forever into the horizon.

I thought I saw **something moving there.** Whatever it was, **it was big,** but I saw it for only a second—then the clouds blocked my view.

Had I **imagined** it?

I **tore** my gaze away.

I didn't have time to dwell on anything except trying to **survive.**
I realized I had no **Feather Falling** effect, which was required to survive
landing after such a jump.

I glanced around, looking for a nearby pool, a canal. **<u>Anything.</u>**
As luck would have it, the roof on one of our wells had been taken
down. Maybe the builders were about to repair it, or maybe some **noob**
had come into the village and taken it. It seemed like a better spot to
land than in the middle of some **farmer's crop.**

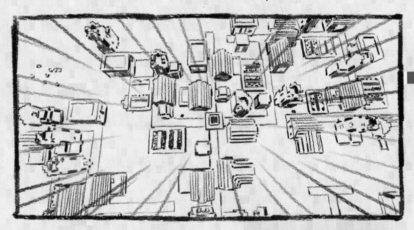

Falling, **falling, falling.** This is
how it feels to be a raindrop.

Falling, falling, falling.

Faster than the prices at my bottle
shop.

I'd never been **this afraid** before.

The kind of terror where time seems to **slow down** and the color drains from your vision. The whole thing **had a dream-like quality.** One moment, I'm about to show a punk from school why I'm the **number-two student.** The next, I'm flying through the clouds, where even bats won't go . . .

I suppose
these things happen.

First, the good news:
I survived.

Didn't take **a single heart's worth of damage**. On top of that, I got **a new record book** and still have **seventeen emeralds left over**. Apparently, after I jumped **over eighty blocks up**, the rest of our bottles sold out in less than a minute.

RUNT
STUDENT
LEVEL 52

MINING	25%
COMBAT	30%
TRADING	100%
FARMING	39%
BUILDING	71%
CRAFTING	45%

75

I felt whole again, and I breathed a **sigh of relief.**

How long has it been since I'd last seen this? **Eight days? Nine?** Well, it felt like **forever.** I was **happy** to see that my level had jumped almost as high as I had jumped last night.

On to the bad news. I had just arrived at school, right?

Went to the head teacher, plunked down **fifty emeralds** for the book, and was on my way to class, right?

Then I noticed some **creepy-looking** guy following me.

He was trying to act **all normal,** but come on—how many older guys in **black robes and sunglasses** do you see walking around a school like mine? I whistled merrily to myself, trying to look **innocent.** Didn't help. He kept following me down the hall. **I walked faster.** So did he, until he caught up.

"A bit windy today," he said. "The clouds sure are . . . *zooming across the sky.*"

"Hurrn. That's interesting. Excuse me."

I zoomed off down a hallway, through a few doors.

Lost him, I thought. So, what is this? He's an elder, certainly. Does he want to talk to me about yesterday?

Another one soon approached.

"Good day, Runt. I've heard your scores are . . . really up there. Why, yes, why I'd say you're . . . flying high."

"Thanks," I said. "Really. It's nice of you to say that."

I turned around to make another run for it, but the first guy was there, blocking my way.

"Come with us," said the guy without glasses. "Immediately."

Thirty minutes later, I was on the other side of the village—in a cobblestone building with iron doors and iron bars for windows. This place was not a jail, however. It was like a hangout spot for a bunch of old, cranky guys who called themselves elders. They led me to a small, featureless room and . . .

offered me some pumpkin pie.

And so began my wonderful day. I guess soaring through the sky has its downsides. Mostly, these guys wanted to know how I had managed to do it. (*Actually, everyone in the village wants to know that, including Steve and Mike.*) As if I could tell them.

"I crafted a **Potion of Leaping II**," was all I could say.

"Sounds like you crafted a **Potion of Leaping One Billion**," the guy with black sunglasses said.

"Look, Runt. **My name is Brio**, and I simply want to ask you a few questions about yesterday's . . . **incident.**"

By **"a few questions,"** he meant **over one thousand questions.**

Stuff like,

"So how *exactly* did you put the **glowstone dust** into the brewing stand?"

"Which hand did you **grab** the potion with?"

"Did the glowstone dust have a **funny smell?**"

"What was the weather like during that exact moment?"

"Can you remember the specific pattern of clouds?"

"Was the sun behind a cloud?"

"Would you like some more pumpkin pie?"

"Were there any **chickens** around?"

"How about some cookies?"

"Can you show us, **precisely,** how you crafted the potion? Re-create your exact movements?"

I blinked.

"We'd . . . need a brewing stand for that."

Brio pointed to the other guy.

"Pretend he's the brewing stand."

Right. After they were done asking questions, I had one of my own.

"Brio. Yesterday, I thought I saw **something walking** in that strange forest."

"Oh?"

"Yeah. The thing **was huge.** Almost as tall as the trees."

"Probably **shadows** playing tricks on your eyes," he said.

"But . . ."

"Or maybe it was a zombie?" He patted me on the head.

"Who knows?"

Yeah. He totally brushed me off. It only got **worse** from there. When Brio finally let me go, he gave me a book. It's **the second schoolbook** for this year.

MINECRAFT
GOLDEN RULES
HANDBOOK

NOOBVILLE

VOLUME 2

The teachers had handed it out today, but since I wasn't at school . . .

"Finish it by tonight," Brio said. "You might find some good tips in there."

This is **cruel** and **unusual** punishment, man, I thought.

After today, I'm never going to drink a potion
again.

Well, Steve went **boom** today.

I guess he finally saw **Urf's books.** The whole front cover with him **riding a pig,** in a mine cart, on his way to **"Noobtown"** *(of which he is supposedly the mayor)* was just too much for him.

So he **quit.** He's been wanting to experiment with **redstone** anyway, he said. The mayor will have him working on that stuff from now on. Of course, Urf was overjoyed. He figured he was going to get his old job back.

Sadly, the head teacher wanted to try someone new.

I say **sadly** because . . . . I'd rather have Urf than this new combat teacher. **Drill** is his name.

He's an elder, like Urf. But one hundred times **grumpier.** The first part of his combat class was sprinting **fifteen laps** around the field. That wouldn't have been too bad, but he dug holes all around the edge of the combat field and filled them with water.

Seriously,
this guy is crazy.

"MOVE, YOU ENDERMITES!! I'VE SEEN ZOMBIES SWIM FASTER UP WATERFALLS!!"

It was **the most intense** combat class I've ever had. After running, we had to swing at practice dummies **five hundred times.** Stump, Max, and I started beating away at the same dummy. Drill rushed over.

"I SAID GROUPS OF TWO!!" he screamed, and glared at me. "YOU!! WITH HER!!" Then he pointed at her. **Breeze.** She'd chosen a practice dummy near mine, of course—and of course, she was all by herself.

I could tell it was going to be **one of those weeks.**

"But they're my friends," I said.

"WHAT DID YOU JUST SAY, YOU SQUID-BRAINED POTATO JOCKEY?!"

Potato jockey?! That's like a chicken jockey, except . . . riding a potato.

I tried to **imagine** someone riding a pig-size potato and couldn't. **Just couldn't.** The very attempt **hurt my brain.** Then I got **angry.** **Who's he calling a potato jockey?!**

"I **said**, they're my—"

Let me just make this clear: That was a bad choice of words.

No, let me be more clear: **Any** choice of words would have been a bad choice of words.

Drill got **so angry** he couldn't even speak in full sentences, just single words that sputtered out of his mouth:

"GIVE!! ME!! F-FIFTY!!"

Sigh. After the push-ups, I gave my friends a shrug and joined Breeze.

"Hey."

"Hey."

Whatever. It could have been worse. I could have gotten paired with one of Pebble's friends, or that **Bumbi** kid.

So Breeze and I swung our swords **in silence.** My arms already felt like anvils from all the push-ups, so I **slowed down** whenever Drill left our area and **sped up** when he came back.

Breeze was different. She swung at **a steady rate,** whether Drill was there or not. In fact, come to think of it, she was one of the **few students** Drill never shouted at. Even though she never did anything **amazing** in class, she never drew the anger of the teachers, either. Even this teacher, who freaked out over the tiniest thing.

In other words, Breeze was invisible
—neither good nor bad—
a completely <u>average</u> student.

That was why I'd never really noticed her until she started **following me around.** I mean, I've never seen her use any **fancy** moves—like that time I landed that huge critical hit and made the dummy's head fly off and roll on the ground with Steve clapping and telling me **good job** afterward. *(I'm proud of that one. Can you tell?)*

Later on, everyone moved to the **archery range.**

I'll just be up front: I'm a terrible shot with a bow. Give me a big sword and I'll show you bigger crits. Give me a bow, however, and you're endangering your own life, and everyone else's, including mine. How does someone hit themselves with their own arrows? I don't know, but I'm sure **I could do it.**

Here's some proof:

This was my shot while standing **still**, with a motionless target, from **thirty blocks away.**

Basically, if you need someone to hit a fully grown ghast at a range of ten blocks, well, **I'm your guy.** I'm totally your guy. *As long as the ghast isn't moving.* Outside of that, all I can really do with a bow is **scare mobs** with the whistling noise the arrows make.

Oh, now it's eleven blocks away. Aim carefully.

Breeze did great, though. **At first,** anyway. The first five arrows she shot were all **dead center.** Two were so close, the second arrow **split the first in half.** That's something I've only seen in storybooks at the library, with **some crazy villager dressed all in green.**

"**Wow.**" I glanced at her, at the wool target, then back to her. "You're amazing."

"**Not really,**" she said, shaking her head. Her cheeks were pink. "Just luck."

Maybe it *was* just luck.

Because after that, she never managed to hit red again.

So strange.
Maybe I made her nervous.

With ten minutes left until the end of class, we had to do another **fifteen laps** around the field. It started pouring rain. A few kids complained. A streak of anger flashed across Drill's face, and his voice boomed like thunder:

"YOU THINK THE MOBS ARE GONNA CARE ABOUT YOUR FEELINGS?! MOVE, YOU CREEPER-FACED ENDERBABIES!! MOVE!!"

Nice.
Just think—tomorrow,
I get to do this all over again.

SPECIAL
UPDATE

I just **woke up** in the middle of the night from a **crazy dream.** I'm going to write down everything I can remember:

In the dream, Steve had built some **huge redstone contraption.**

"It's **a vending machine,**" he said. "We have them back on Earth."

"And what does it do?" I asked.

"In this case, you **drop an emerald into the hopper** here, select which **potion** you want, and the potion comes out of the dispenser there."

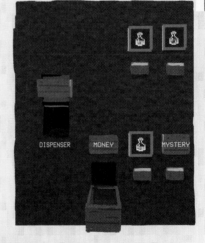

"What kind of potions?"

"**Well,** they're not really potions so much as **flavored drinks.**"

"Flavored drinks?"

"Never mind."

I studied the strange machine.

"What happens if you put in something **besides an emerald?**"

"It **rejects** it. Or **eats** it, but that only happens sometimes. It's a work in progress."

"It can recognize what kind of item you put into it? **Is that even possible with redstone?**"

For a second, Steve's eyes had an almost **opalescent** shimmer.

"With enough hard work, **anything is possible,** Runt."

I glanced at the button on the lower right:

Mystery . . .

"What does this button do?"

"Maybe you should find out."

Hurrrn. I pressed the button. The scene faded. **Darkness.**

"Please help me," the **wither skeleton** said. "I'm stranded on a lava island."

"Why would I help you? You're a mob. **You're a noob mob,** too. Wither skeletons are immune to lava, **aren't they?** So just swim to shore."

"**But not all of us are bad.** Surely you know that. Also, I can't swim. Please build a bridge for me. If you help me, I'll . . . **help you.**"

"Help me how?"

"There's someone you **need to meet.**"

"**Whatever.** This is *my* dream. Go away."

"Right now, I might be just a part of your dream . . . but we will **meet in the future.**"

" . . ."

"By the way," the wither skeleton said, **"tell Jello I said, 'Hi.'"**

Darkness. Then I was in an unfamiliar house.

Three kids—two girls and a boy—were sitting at a table.

"Who are you guys?" I asked.

"I'm **Skyler,**" said one girl.

"**Katie,**" said the other.

The boy smiled. "**Ben.**"

The girl named Skyler **stood up.** "Notch sent us into your dream to give you a message," she said. She pointed out the window.

"They'll be here soon.

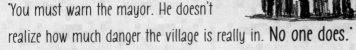

"You must warn the mayor. He doesn't realize how much danger the village is really in. **No one does.**"

I glanced out the window again.

"So . . . **the trees are coming for us?**"

Ben approached the window, too.

"No, not the *trees*. **Them.** Isn't it obvious?"

"Who?!"

"You aren't too bright, are you, Runt?"

That came from Katie, who was behind me, now. All three began pointing out the window. **"Look again!"**

The grass under the trees began rustling. Yet . . . everything else was **absolutely still.** Not even the clouds moved. There was an **eerie** feeling. It made me sick to my stomach. Then the whole world **shook** slightly. There was **a horrible roaring** sound far in the distance.

"It's him!" said Ben.

"Yes! He's here!"

"Who?!" I shouted.

Skyler turned to face me.

"Runt! Listen! **Remember** what you saw when you were—"

The scene cut away. Again, darkness. A man appeared in the inky gloom. He looked like Steve, yet there was something **creepy** about him. He . . . **had no eyes.** Or, rather, his eyes were white. And glowing. White light emerged behind him, and smoke, as if from a massive fire.

Something was **burning.**

"I'm . . . coming for you . . ."

The **roaring** sound came back again, deafening this time.

The man's eyes grew **brighter and brighter** until everything was white.

"Wuah!!!"

I sat up in bed, wide-awake, and remained like that for a while. An **eerie feeling** lingered on the edge of my mind. Those three kids said Notch sent them into my dream . . . Is something like that possible? Are they from Earth? Maybe they play that *Minecraft* game, like Steve and Mike used to. Is our village really in so much **danger?** We haven't had a mob attack in quite some time.

And who was that guy with the glowing white eyes? He <u>didn't seem very friendly</u>.

After I brushed off the fear, I opened up **Jello's item chest** and fed him some bread.

"You don't happen to know a wither skeleton, do you, Jello?"

I petted him. He was **cool to the touch**.

"No, of course you don't. **It was just a dream.**"

91

SPECIAL
UPDATE

There was a **huge meeting** this morning. The mayor **finally** talked to everyone about the **ever-encroaching forest.**

"As you are all aware, a vast number of **dark oak trees** have been growing in the east," he said. "This area is considered **dangerous.** Sunlight won't reach the mobs there, which means they **can travel around during the day.** We're currently experimenting with ways to deal with this problem, should the trees grow too **close to the village.**

"**Don't be alarmed.** We've survived many attacks in the past, and we'll survive so many more. This is simply the next step in the mobs' strategy, and it's **a very obvious one.**"

Brio—*the guy with black sunglasses*—**joined** the mayor at the oak block.

"From now on, the students will face **more and more difficult classes,** harsher training, and . . . each student must **submit an idea** to help protect our village. This will be your **final test** before you graduate."

The mayor nodded.

"Students, you must **train your hardest.** The mobs are improving quickly, it seems. So must we. I've noticed **petty squabbles** between some of you, and I suggest you end them today. The real enemy lies beyond those walls, **not within.**"

That was pretty much it. So, the trees allow mobs to **hide** from the sunlight. Zombies and skeletons can **move around during the day**, as long as they stay within that forest.

But is there more to it than that?
Skyler, Ben, and Katie
seemed to think so.

Hmm.

Later, in combat class, I had to be **partners with Breeze** *again.*

I got to enjoy another hour of being screamed at by Drill, crawling through mud, and **a weird girl** as my partner. Max and Stump have been having a blast in comparison.

Needless to say, it's been the **worst week of my life.**

It soon got worse. Brio and the mayor observed the combat class today, from a distance. After class, Drill **spoke** with the mayor.

Drill said that Breeze and I are **such good partners,** we should work together *every* class . . . .

That teacher is too mean.
<u>Too mean.</u>

Call me a potato jockey: okay, that's fine, I can roll with that. But working with Breeze every day until I graduate?! **What is this?! Such cruelty! Such pain!**

I complained to the head teacher, but that was **useless.** He likes Breeze. He thinks she's a great student. When I mentioned how weird she is, he didn't believe me—in fact, he gave me the **"Runt just invited me to a slumber party in the Nether"** look.

Why does **everyone** give me that look?!

Why <u>!!!</u>

"Come on, it'll be fun!! Bring your own beds!!"

The weird dreams came back tonight. This time, it was the events of Sunday—**in reverse.** So, in a way, it wasn't so much a *dream* as it was me **remembering** things. There wasn't much sound while the scenes played out, just an eerie static or buzzing noise.

Creepy, right?

I tried **my best** to remember what I saw that day.

It was like a zombie, or a skeleton . . . something standing upright
. . . **except it was huge.**

It was almost as **tall as the dark oaks.** Not even endermen are
that tall. What was it? I couldn't make it out **clearly.** It was too far
away, and my **eyes were all watery** from the wind. I soon began
dreaming for real:

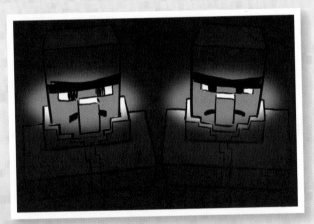

Nonono.
NNNNNNo.

This dream is **not** turning into a nightmare. **Come on, Runt.** This
is **your dream.** You're the boss in here. Control this thing.

There we go! Now this is a dream!

Yeeeeahhh!!

I don't wanna wake up!

Breeze was such a noob today.

My new **"partner"** did almost everything wrong. One of her potions even **exploded** in brewing class. Afterward, she just blinked, sneezed, and said, **"Oops."**

"Wow," Pebble said, "looks like you **two noobs** are made for each other." Almost everyone in class **laughed.**

Max and Stump gave me a guilty look. At least *they* were having fun . . .

Anyway, I had to **get away** from her. So, during lunch, I took off to the school library. I couldn't stop thinking about what I had seen in the forest, anyway, and wanted to do some research.

Mungo the Overlord was the **biggest mob** I'd
read about. Thinking back, the thing I had spotted on
Sunday could have been a huge zombie. I remember
reading about giant zombies. **They were super rare.**

Fast-forward an hour: I didn't find any mobs, even
legendary ones, in the library's books that fit what I
had seen. Afternoon classes went by in a blur. I didn't
even pay attention to Drill's shouts; I just did my push-
ups, ran my laps. He was a bit hard to ignore, though.

**"I'VE SEEN SILVERFISH CRAWL THROUGH COBBLESTONE FASTER
THAN YOU!!"**

 After school, I told Steve about my sighting.
He laughed it off.

"Probably just a **cow.** There might be a few zombies
out there, but that's it."

The mayor said the same thing.

"You want me to **modify my plans** because you think you saw
something?"

Stump also blew me off.

"Lay off the potions, dude. Really." His blue eyes, normally
cheerful, were filled with **worry.**

99

"Can't you just be a normal kid and stop getting into trouble? What happened to just studying hard and becoming warriors?"

Hurrrg.

(I haven't had a good old-fashioned hurrrg in a while.)

However, when I mentioned my dream to Max, he nodded slowly.

"I saw something, too," he said. "Heard something, rather. The other night. My dad and I had an argument, so I stepped outside and went for a walk. Went to the east wall. Something **moaned so loud** out there I had trouble sleeping when I went back home."

"So I'm not the only one, then."

"How about we go find out?"

"What are you talking about?"

"I say we head over there tomorrow night," Max said. "Just sneak out of the village and go find out what's in there."

"Are you crazy?!"

"Maybe. After all, what **sane** person would ever want to fight mobs for a living?"

Stump's words came back to haunt me: *(Can't you just be a normal kid and stop getting into trouble? What happened to just studying hard and becoming warriors?)*

I told Max that I didn't want to do anything **crazy** anymore.

"Besides," I said, "if the mayor ever found out about this . . ."

"He won't find out," Max said. He clapped his hands together. **"It's like this, Runt.** Let's say the mayor's right, and there's nothing out there except some zombies. Maybe a skeleton or two. Then we won't be in any danger at all. I've got some **Potions of Invisibility.** We'll be totally fine. However, if the mayor's wrong and we're right, then **the village really <u>needs to know.</u>"**

I couldn't believe this kind of stuff was coming from Max . . .

But what came next—

"I love my village," he said, "and I'm prepared to take **minor risks** to help the people I love.

My family.
My friends.

"The little kids that play in the street near my house. I'm not gonna let the mobs get them."

He had **a kind of strength** when he said this, a confidence I'd never seen in anyone else, not even Steve—it was **impossible** not to feel moved. And at that point, I understood: **these are the words of a warrior.**

I stood up straighter.
Nodded.
<u>Even smiled.</u>

We **crept** out of the village after the sun went down.

The east wall of the village didn't have a gate, but there was a **secret trapdoor** that allowed easy passage. We crept through the tunnel and exited into the plains.

Max **wasn't kidding** when he said he had **Potions of Invisibility.** He'd been stockpiling them. I didn't ask where he'd gotten **so many golden nuggets.** Even **a single potion** had a **pretty steep price**—eight per potion, plus a fermented spider eye—yet Max handed me **five** without batting an eye.

"How long do these potions last?" I asked.

"They're extended," Max said. **"Eight-minute duration."**

At **five** potions each, we had **forty minutes** to snoop around. We chugged a bottle each. At first, it **was difficult walking** without seeing our legs or hands. The closer we got to the dark forest, the more my heart sank into my stomach. **There was no sound** beyond the soft crunching of grass underneath our feet.

"This way," Max said. **"The valley.** See it?"

"Yeah."

We crept forward, **slowly, slowly.**

I could hear him breathing, and he could no doubt hear me.

Both of us <u>were afraid.</u>

"At least this place still has animals," I whispered, pointing. "Maybe it's **not so bad** here?"

"Quiet."

"What is it?"

"Listen."

We stood there for a long time—*at least a minute, although it seemed like forever*—invisible, **barely breathing.**

Then Max's footsteps **broke** the silence.

"Let's go."

We stepped into the forest. It was gloomy, hard to see, and I regretted not bringing some potions of my own—**Night Vision.**

"Saplings," I said.

"Let's keep going."

We **crept** forward, **waited, listened, looked around**, and when we felt we had two minutes left on our invisibility, we drank another potion each—**just to be safe.**

At one point, I thought I heard a crunching sound.

I bumped into Max, almost knocking him over.

"Forward," he said. **"Real slow."**

We moved forward, past some big trees . . .

And then—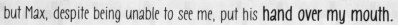

I almost screamed—

but Max, despite being unable to see me, put his **hand over my mouth.**

He grabbed me, and we both **backed up,** until the mobs were out of sight and only the crunching **sounds of the shovel** could still be heard. **This is insane,** Max whispered.

"The mobs . . . they . . ."

I was thinking the same thing.

I . . . can't believe it. The **mobs** made **this forest?** A skeleton was holding a shovel. A zombie was holding a sapling. But . . . they're **mobs! Not villagers! Not Earth kids!** Not noobs, or warriors, or even iron golems, who often hold flowers the same way that zombie was holding that baby tree—**so delicately,** with the utmost care.

That zombie was acting like he didn't want to damage the sapling's roots. **He probably had a respectable Farming score.**

Mobs!!

With Farming scores?!?!

Mobs that know how to farm?!

How can they . . . how did they . . . **they've been planting trees?!**

How?! How is that even possible?!

What, they've got farming classes over there in **Mob City,** do they?!

I mean, I assumed this forest would be crawling with them, but to think that they actually created—

Boom!
Boom!!
Boom!!!

The ground was **shaking** slightly. A **massive** creature shambled toward the skeleton and the zombie.

It must have stood at least **six blocks high.** Its fists were **one block across;** its head was slightly bigger than that.

My scientific calculations concluded that this could mean only one thing:

RUNRUNRUNRUN
RUNRUNRUNRUN.

Max and I made it back in one piece. None of the mobs **noticed us.** Not even **the big guy** with tree trunks for arms. We found Stump and told him everything. Of course, none of us had seen or heard of a mob like that. **We wanted to know what it was.**

Max suggested we try to find more information in a library. The three of us headed to the biggest library in the village and began looking through a bunch of ancient, **dusty** books.

Breeze slipped into the library shortly thereafter. She entered when two other kids were leaving to prevent me from noticing her. But I saw her thin form—*like a blurred shadow in the dim corner of the library*—just as she zoomed behind an aisle of books.

Max eventually **found** what we were looking for. A librarian can come in handy, after all. It was a book with a simple green cover and an even simpler name:

Legendary Mobs of Minecraftia.

Despite its **boring** outward appearance, this book was filled with a lot of **crazy stuff.** It's an encyclopedia of legendary mobs—**boss monsters,** as they're referred to on Earth. Well, the three of us sat around and **flipped through its chapters.**

By the way, all of the mobs in this book were **100% real.** Some of them sounded downright **terrifying,** such as **the screaming cow** *(all living things close enough to hear its cries get the wither debuff).*

Or **the obsidian giant** *(it's nearly twenty blocks tall and the only weapon that can harm it is a diamond pickaxe).*

Then I found one that sent **<u>a chill</u>** down my spine.

URKK
DOOMWHIP

"That's our mob," I said.

Stump seemed **skeptical.**

"You're sure? Maybe it was an enderman?"

"**No,** this thing was no enderman," Max said. "Every time it walked, it created a **mini earthquake.**"

"Well, if this guy's really out there," Stump said, "**then this village is in big trouble.** Says here **Urkk** is a **midlevel boss mob.** Can take out iron golems without even trying and **hurl creepers up to fifteen blocks** for a ranged explosive attack. This ability has earned him the nickname

'The Creeper Express.'"

. . .
. . .
. . .

Everyone fell **silent** for a moment, considering these words. Max then read aloud from the book.

First, Urkk **is seven blocks tall.** He's got special bone armor made from the bones of **wither skeletons.**

(The book estimates that this guy has maybe **three times the life-force of an iron golem.**) That's a lot of hearts. But the **craziest** thing about him is **his weapon:** a modified fishing rod—**a special, unique item.** How he crafted it is still a mystery to Minecraftian sages.

It has a longer reach than a normal fishing rod with a fast-flying hook. But what makes this fishing rod truly deadly are the **Pulling II**

URKK'S
HOOK
PULLING II
SHARPNESS VII

and **Sharpness VII** enchantments, meaning it pulls hooked targets **closer** and deals an **incredible amount of damage** when it does.

"I didn't even know a **seventh level** of Sharpness **existed**," Breeze said. All three of us looked up at her in **surprise**. *(Even though I had seen her enter, I'd already forgotten about her.)*

Max shrugged. "Boss mobs like this tend to have **crazy items and abilities.**"

The **fear** snuck up on my heart like a creeper that had drunk a Potion of Invisibility. "How can we **defend** ourselves against this guy?" I asked.

Max shrugged again. "Don't get hooked?"

"Come on," I said. "There has to be something else."

Stump pointed at the bottom of the right page. "**He has a phobia.**"

"**Huh?**" I said.

"What's that?" Max asked.

"It's another word for **fear**," Stump said. "You know how creepers are **afraid of cats?** Skeletons, dogs? Well, he's got one, too.

"He's afraid of heights."

"Interesting." Max read some more. "So, he's terrified of any vertical drop greater than **five blocks.**"

Suddenly, Stump rose from his chair. "What are we doing here?! We're just sitting around talking! We've gotta go **warn the mayor!**"

I figured the mayor would just brush us off, but we had to try. Max grabbed the *Legendary Mobs* book and off we went to the mayor's house.

The sound of a distant explosion echoed through the streets— and then there was a distant roar, which could have only come from that **gigantic pigman, Urkk.**

I drew my wooden sword, remembering Max's words.

Friends. Family. The little kids who play in the street. No mobs are going to get them.

This giant noob named **Urkk** is going down.

Ever been in a big village **just before sunset?**

Ever watched all the villagers **scrambling around,** desperately trying to get home before the sun went down? Well, after the **explosions**, our village was like that. **Only in reverse.**

And with a lot of screaming.

Despite weeks of **intense training**, we just weren't prepared.

It was **total chaos.**

Smoke was rising in the east, and almost no one wanted to stick around for the mobs' little surprise party.

Well, some did. Some were actually running *toward* the smoke, like fish swimming upstream. My friends and I fell into that last category. **Call us brave. Call us foolish, or foolhardy, or simply fools.**

Call us whatever you want to, but we were determined to crash that party. The thing is our anger toward the mobs goes back a long way—

way before the slime bombings. All those years of living in fear, unable to sleep, listening to the spiders shrieking, the skeletons rattling . . .

We'd had **enough.**

We'd decided that we just weren't going to **put up with it** anymore.

I won't provide a detailed narrative for this battle—not too many *he saids, she saids, I did this, he did that.*

To be **honest,** I can't remember much. It was just a blur.

In those first moments, I, like everyone else, was struggling to accept the cold, hard reality: **In broad daylight,** with barely a cloud in the sky, the mobs had launched the biggest attack in the history of the village.

SATURDAY: BATTLE—PART TWO

The first thing I noticed was . . . **the zombies weren't burning in the sunlight.** There they were, shambling in the distance, without so much as a spark emitting from them. It was their **armor.** Some were **fully suited in leather;** a few were even in **iron.**

Regardless of what they wore, though, every single one was equipped with *at least* **a helmet.**

(Some zombies wore a helmet and a pair of boots without a tunic or leggings, which was just bizarre.)

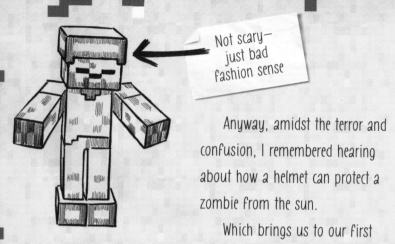

Not scary—
just bad
fashion sense

Anyway, amidst the terror and confusion, I remembered hearing about how a helmet can protect a zombie from the sun.

Which brings us to our first interesting point: A zombie wearing *any* sort of armor is **quite rare, let alone an *army* of zombies wearing armor.**

Consider how much work it must have taken to outfit them all. I mean, have you ever tried crafting a full suit of leather armor? It's **an epic quest.** You need, like, **fifty cows,** which means feeding cows over and over for what seems like forever—and the whole time, you're listening to that endless **mooing** and wondering if you have enough wheat: you're going out to check your crops at night, thinking, *Are those torches close enough, should I use bone meal, should I gather more seeds, should I go to those plains over there and take out some horses for* **extra** *leather*—until finally, you stop farming for leather altogether and go into a cave, because why not? The truth is you could get **iron faster.**

By the way, that's just for *one* set of **leather armor.** How about **one *hundred*?** That's the estimated number of zombies, in full leather, **that attacked our village today.**

Knowing that, one must ask: **Where did they get the materials?** It meant they were farming cows. It meant, somewhere in Minecraftia, there was a cow farm—a farm quite possibly the size of our entire village—tended by various mobs. It also meant they were **mining** and **smelting iron.** Not only did they have the resources for such a massive number of items, but they knew how to craft them as well. So—they probably have zombie **blacksmiths.** Zombie **miners.** Zombie **butchers.** Zombie **armorers.** Zombie **crafters.** Zombie **builders.** Zombie **cooks.** Zombie **bakers.** Zombie advanced **redstone engineers.** **Zombie every possible profession** **you could possibly** **ever think of.**

And why stop at zombies? Somewhere out there, there's probably a **charged creeper lumberjack.**

Meet **Creepojack**.
He's so manly he swings his axe with his teeth. HIS TEETH. And when his axe finally breaks, he just explodes, providing easy harvesting for the next guy.

Nothing would surprise me anymore. But hey, all this is just preparing me for **the real world**, you know? At least this way, if I ever see a slime fisherman, I won't freak out, or be shocked, or offend him by asking how a slime could possibly be a fisherman since he has no arms. Instead, I'll just plunk down next to him, whip out my own fishing rod, and ask if he's had any bites. **Skeleton librarians.** **Enderman shepherds.** I could accept all that.

There was one possibility I couldn't, though: What if some of those zombies have **a better combat score than I do?**

Zombie . . . warriors?

No way!!

I refuse to believe it!!

With sudden anger,
I cut into a zombie with my wooden sword.

SATURDAY: BATTLE—PART THREE

This, of course, brings us to our next point.
You see, after I **attacked that zombie,**
well, it attacked *me.*
Who knew?

116

Let me tell you, that single moment was **worth more** than two or three days' worth of Intro to Combat. Steve is a **great teacher,** don't get me wrong, and that Drill guy scares me to no end, but that zombie gave me a hands-on lesson in just how **strong** zombies actually are. My vision flashed bright **red.** A wave of pain flooded my senses. **The life bar in the bottom of my vision reduced by two hearts.**

The **courage** I'd felt just moments ago **vanished** like an enderman in the rain, like water in **the Nether,** like mushrooms in sunlight, like a waterfall after someone scooped up the spring block with a bucket.

(Actually, that last example is a bit slow, isn't it? Gah. Never mind.)

Anyway, I was **knocked back** from the sheer force of the zombie's attack.

Just then, a **horrifying** thought hit me: **Real.** This is real. I'm **20%** closer to vanishing in a **puff** of smoke. If I make too many mistakes—if I let Mr. Stinkypants remove every last heart from my life bar—**that's it.**

After that, I felt impossibly **heavy** and **cold.** An anvil in my stomach and ice blocks in my veins. For a moment, **Intro to Combat** went right out the window. So did Sir Runt, the word *warrior,* and everything in between. **I forgot everything.**

Everything I'd ever learned, everything that Steve had ever taught me, and everything Drill had ever drilled into my head—gone, like **an enchanted diamond** sword accidentally dropped into lava.

In fact, I . . . <u>almost ran</u>.

In my defense, the number of mobs out there was enough to make an iron golem cry.

In the words of Urf: **"This is baadddd."** He said this in a deep, **terrified voice.** (In addition, he made a deep grunting sound before saying this, which I cannot replicate with words or letters. Perhaps something similar to what a pigman might sound like when struck in the butt by lightning.) Then he ran into a nearby house and peeked out a window with **the most ridiculous expression** on his face. He reminded me of a creeper that had to go to the bathroom really bad.

In contrast, Drill was at his **angriest.** Somewhere in the distance, he was **shouting so loud** my ears hurt even from where I was standing. **"HOLD THE LINE, YOU RABBIT JOCKEYS!! GET IN FORMATION!!"**

Whatever. No one was listening to him. Everyone was too shaken, too confused, and way too **preoccupied.**

It was like this **everywhere** you looked. Kids from school, the **best of friends,** fighting back to back as zombies trudged endlessly forward.

Chris and Kevin.

Joanne and Jamie, twin sisters.

And fighting in one big group: **Kristen, Brennan, Marco, Beth, Jackson, Jenn, Tanesha**, and a kid nicknamed **CamouflageBoy.** They all fought **valiantly,** oblivious to Drill's shouts. Besides, no matter how many times he ordered us to "**hold the line,**" there was simply no line to hold. Zombies were **everywhere.**

Things looked really grim. Until Stump **freaked out,** that is.

"I hope you brought **an anvil,**" he said to a zombie, "because you're gonna need it to repair your face ten times after this!!"

With a loud cry, he slammed the zombie back **again and again.**

The zombie actually tried to run . . . before it crumbled into **light gray dust.**

Experience orbs flew from the pile, into my friend, who then swung his sword around slowly in the air.

Kids cheered as if he'd just slain **the ender dragon** itself. It was enough to bring me to my senses and **respawn** several weeks of combat classes in my mind. This time, when a zombie lunged for me, I stepped back and swung my blade. When he staggered back, **I dashed forward and swung again.**

Three swings later, I defeated my first mob.

After the zombie fell, I felt a **slight surge of energy** from the experience flying into me.

Max dropped his own zombie at about the same time. He **muttered something** about how slaying his first mob wasn't as cool as it had sounded in the adventure books he'd read.

All around me, more and more villagers were doing the same. We were pushing them back. *(Well, technically, we were chopping them or slashing them.)* Morale only increased when **Mike showed up.** "I saw that," he said to Stump. "**Nice work,** kid, but don't get too reckless, huh? Same goes for you two."

"Okay, hurrr."

"You got it, Mike."

"Don't worry. We'll be **careful.**"

The warrior gave us **the strangest** look.

"Man, what *are* you guys? **The Three Muskanoobs?**"

I returned the expression.

"**Um, what?**"

"Never mind."

Hurrrgg.

I was still trying to remember all **the weird words** Steve had taught me, and now *Mike* was using them, too. Max seemed equally annoyed.

"Honestly," he said, "if any more of you guys show up in our village, we're gonna need **a class on Earth slang.**"

SATURDAY: BATTLE—PART FOUR

The third point I'll bring up is perhaps the most **interesting** *(to me, at least).*

Tactics. Not ours, mind you. Our tactics mostly consisted of **screaming, trembling, shaking,** and randomly **freaking out.**

But the mobs had it down. As a **warrior-in-training,** I'll admit it: the way they moved was beautiful. Even Drill was **impressed,** shouting something about how he wanted to switch sides instead of commanding a bunch of **no-good, carrot-brained** dirt farmers.

Here's the most common trick the mobs pulled. We're calling it the **"zombie shuffle."** Basically, the zombies seemed to realize that they were **the least valuable**, the most worthless. So they'd make a formation in front of the skeletons. They were shielding the skeletons with their own bodies.

The technical term here is <u>meat shields.</u>

But it didn't end there. Sometimes, the skeletons **hissed** in an unknown language. *(That language is the ancient tongue, by the way, like the words found on enchanting tables.)* Then the zombies **moved** to the side slightly, giving the skeletons enough room to **shoot** arrows at us.

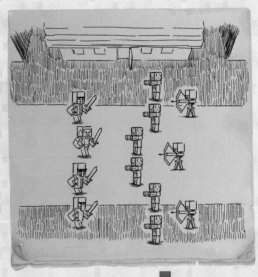

If anyone tried to **close in on a skeleton**, the zombies moved back, **blocking** their path.

Unbelievable, right? At least, **Mike couldn't believe it:**

"So they're using formations now?! Is this even *Minecraft?!*"

Max **blocked** an arrow with his sword.

"Welcome to our world, buddy boy."

Of course, the mobs had many more tricks up their sleeves.

Once, a single spider carried **five skeletons** up a house, one by one.

A few zombies carried **axes** and chopped holes in walls to launch **surprise attacks**.

One zombie even had **flint** and **steel** and set fire to everything he could. A lot of houses were lost today.

The craziest mob trick, however, was the "**zombie sandwich.**" When we first saw it, we didn't know what to think.

What *is* **a zombie sandwich, you ask?**

How can you make one? What are the ingredients?

Here's **the recipe:**

Step 1: Take **three to five** creepers.

Step 2: Surround those creepers with **eight to eleven zombies.**

Step 3: Just cry.

They moved together as **a single unit,** which meant that we had a hard time taking down the creepers before they **blew up.** When those creepers started **hissing** and **flashing,** all we could do was move back. They pulled this off a few times, whenever they wanted to blow up a certain building . . . or take out a group of iron golems.

Incredibly, the zombies **moved away** before the creepers went off, **minimizing** their losses.

Meanwhile, a few of us had trouble *holding a sword.*

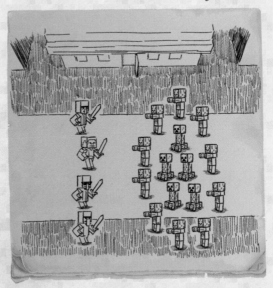

We're never gonna hear the end of this in Intro to Combat.
The Nether will likely freeze over

before Drill's done **scolding** us.

That's not to say we didn't have **tactics** of our own. For example, once, **two zombies** lunged for me at the same time. I managed to knock one back but didn't have time to deal with the second. Then **an arrow** cut through the air, above my right shoulder, and **nailed** the zombie in the arm. It wasn't the **best shot**—*not that I could criticize someone's bow skill*—but it did **knock** the zombie back. I finished the second off before it could recover, then dropped the first and looked around.

Who shot that arrow?
They must be perched **on top** of a house.

Of course.

Even at a time like this, she's still following me around . . .
No matter where I go, **she's there,** somewhere in the background . . .

A crazy fangirl. A creepy stalker. Well, she did **help me out.** Am I being too harsh? **No. No way.**

If she wants to **be friends,** she can talk to me like a **normal person** instead of lurking around like that! Besides, combat class has become **so lame** because of her! If she wasn't always hanging around, Drill would have just let me keep training with **my friends!**

I wish she'd leave me alone!!
I don't need her help!!
<u>Hurrrgg!!</u>

My anger returning, **I cut through a new zombie.**

SATURDAY: BATTLE—PART SIX

While we were fighting, **some girl showed up** and made some flashy moves. Well, she wasn't just **some girl** . . . Her name's **Emerald,** and she's one of **the most popular girls** in school. I've never really talked to her much. **She's kind of annoying. She's** *never* **humble,** occasionally **snide,** often cowardly, and always getting into and out of **jams.**

Despite her somewhat girly appearance, her **bad temper** can be legendary. Max said she outshouted Drill a couple of days ago when he scolded her about something in the street.

After taking out a few mobs, she
turned and **bumped into me.**

"**Sorry.**" She smirked. "You, **um . . .**
kinda got in my way."

"**Sure thing, hurrr.**"

She glanced at the piles of dust.

"So, are you guys holding up?"

"We're getting by."

She nodded.

"By the way, have you seen **Pebble?**"

"No. Here's hoping an iron golem

mistook him for a zombie."

At my response, she made an expression like a cat left out in the
rain. "**Hmmph!** Y'know, he's not so bad."

She **took off** after that. So another one has joined **Team Pebble.**
Anger level: **off the charts.** A zombie approached with a clueless look
on his face. He had no idea what was in store for him. No idea.

I almost felt sorry.

Still, **as angry** as I'd become, I soon cheered up. You see, one of my dreams is to someday wield **a diamond sword.** Diamonds are **super expensive,** right? Well, today was a wonderful opportunity to save up. There were a few **iron golems** roaming around, smacking mobs high into the air. At one point, I just started following a golem around and picking up all the **dropped items.**

Why not? The golem didn't need them. Besides, it was better those items went to *me* instead of **some noob.**

But then, the golem was a bit slow. **Rusty,** perhaps. It would knock a zombie into the air, and I'd have to wait for it to come back down . . . and then wait even longer for the golem to trudge over and do it all again.

Eventually, the golem knocked a zombie onto the roof of a house. The zombie **didn't jump back** down, either. He just glanced around, decided that was that, and sat down. **Urg.** After that, I started following **Mike.** With the way Mike dropped zombies, he was a much more **time-efficient source** of items.

I figured he already had enough **emeralds** and wouldn't mind if I took a few things.

Just a few.

Man,
was I wrong.

He glared at me as if I'd just looted every last item in his **secret
ender chest.**

"Why are you giggling over there, Runt? **It's not funny!** Stop
stealing my items, noob!!"

Tee hee hee.

At some point, **Breeze** jumped down from a house.

She must have **run out of arrows.** But she was **afraid** down here.
She didn't even draw her sword. In fact, I don't even think she *had* one.
What a noob . . .

Several zombies went for her then—*Steve once said they can sense
weakness*—and that was when I **lost it.** I glanced to the right and
shouted:

"What are you doing?! **Get back!!**"

She **tumbled** back before the zombies closed in and hid in an alley.
Since I was distracted, a zombie nearly **struck me.** Claws swiped inches
from my face. I dashed back and shook my head.

What is this?

I was thinking about **her safety** before my own.
Am I starting **to care about her** or something?

Near **the end of the battle,** I noticed something **strange.** I spotted Brio—the guy in all black, with the **black sunglasses.**

He was in **a church tower,** far in the distance.

He was . . . **observing us.** Watching us fight for our lives. Of course, with all the zombies running around, I wasn't able to keep my eyes on him for very long. A few minutes later, **I spotted him again,** on top of the same tower. He jumped down onto the roof of an armory and then into a street, where he slowly walked away. **It gets weirder.**

He went in a direction that was, to my knowledge, totally **overrun** with mobs. A bunch of kids had fled from that area minutes earlier and had warned us **not to go there.** It must have been bad in there, because their faces were so white, as if they'd seen **a ghast.**

Yet I watched as a distant Brio **calmly** strode toward that place, seemingly unafraid—*and without any weapons*—until he vanished behind a house.

130

Seriously **weird.**

What was he doing? Where was he going? I was so **curious** I almost went in there after him. But then I turned back to the battle as a few shouts rose up over the chaos:

"Hey! Look!"

"The mobs are breaking **formation!**"

Drill started screaming at the top of his lungs.

"ALL IN!! NO MERCY!!"

Everyone else screamed just as loudly.

"CHARRRRRRRRRRRRRRRRRRGE!!"

A wave of angry villagers,
led by **an even angrier combat teacher,**
rushed after a **fleeing enemy.**

SATURDAY: BATTLE—PART TEN

Twenty minutes later, the mobs were totally **wiped out.**

An **eerie** silence swept through the streets. Stump sat down and offered me some bread. It was enough to **refill my life bar.**

"Thanks," I said, glancing at him. "You know, you were **amazing** back there."

He shrugged.

"I'm just glad **Urkk** didn't show up."

"Right."

Just then, **Steve walked around a corner**—shambled, really. He was **covered in slime** and dust, his leather armor hung in **tatters,** and he was moving slower than a zombie over soul sand—soul sand with cobwebs placed on top and ice blocks underneath. With a sigh, he tossed his iron sword onto the cobblestone street.

"I'm so done with these mobs."

I rose up.

"Where *were* you?"

"At the square," he said. "They almost pushed through Sunset Lane. You wouldn't believe **how many.**" He slid down a wall, eyes closed. "Looks like they were trying to take the school."

The school?

That didn't make sense to me. Why not the city hall, or the farms, or the storerooms? But I didn't ask any more questions. We were **too tired** to even talk.

The silence was interrupted as a chorus of **shouts** and **cheers** gradually grew louder. At first, I assumed some villagers, and perhaps the mayor, were coming to congratulate us on our victory . . . until I realized what they were shouting. Actually, they were *chanting*. A single word—or rather, **a single name.**

". . . Peh-bull!! Peh-bull!! Peh-bull!!
Peh-bull! Peh-bull!! . . ."

About one **hundred** people then came into view. They were hoisting **Pebble** up over their heads, carrying him down the road, along with that girl **Emerald.**

. . .

There was a wooden clatter as
I threw my own sword **onto the street.**

By Sunday morning, **posters like this** were all you could see:

15 ZOMBIES
8 SKELETONS
5 CREEPERS

1 HERO

Pebble the war hero. The poster boy of the war on mobs. He had apparently killed a total of **fifteen zombies, eight skeletons, five creepers, two spiders, an enderman, and a chicken** *(the chicken was an accident, or so he says).*

An **impressive** number, more than my own, and backed by praise from the mayor, who'd seen it all happen. That girl **Emerald** was praised **even more,** probably because it isn't everyday that you see a horde of zombies taken down by a girl in a light pink robe. **What can I say?** The right place at the right time **and all that.**

In the afternoon, there was a **ceremony** to congratulate all those who had risen up to **defend the village** during the horrible attack.

My friends and I were included in the praise, **of course,** but the two "**heroes**" stole the show. I'm not bitter about that, however. What burns me is how Pebble and Emerald were awarded special cloaks. **Honestly,** they're **the coolest** cloaks I've ever seen, and they're **enchanted** on top of that, granting **protection from fire.**

Everyone else who **took part in** the battle was given a **cloak,** but these items were **trash-tier**—*the kind of item only a noob would get worked up about.*

When I **tried** mine on, Steve said it could have been a **"bib"** . . . whatever *that* is. When I asked him, he said he didn't want to tell me, because I've already been **humiliated** enough today.

On top of that, **Pebble** is now **rank one,** and Emerald is **rank two** . . . Meaning, Max is **third** and I'm **fourth.** Maybe. No one has discovered the identity of that other **high-ranked student,** so who knows. Why can't the teachers just come out with an official ranking system instead of forcing us to guess and peek at one another's record books?

In other news, we told the mayor about **Urkk.** Here's the thing, though. He asked how we **knew about Urkk.**

None of us wanted to get in trouble by admitting we had left the village at night, so we just said we had seen Urkk while we were standing on the wall at night.

"Probably just a cow," the mayor said. "They get pretty big in these parts." He sighed. **"Urkk is a legend,** boys. Nothing more. Mobs like that simply don't exist anymore."

Why did I even try?

(Insert something about the mayor being a noob here.)

I'm so tired of this kind of stuff; I'm currently lacking the **energy** to even come up with a good way to **insult** him. I'll come back to this entry later and fill it in . . .

Lastly,
I'm a little shy to ask, but . . .
what do you think of
my cloak?

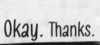

It looks **crooked** because it keeps
bunching up on the left side and no
matter what I do, I can't fix it.

What's that? You said it
looks cool?

Okay. Thanks.
I'll keep wearing it, then.
(By the way, what's a bib?)

MONDAY

There was **no school** today. Due to **the attack,** the mayor thought it would be a good time to establish village **"building codes."** The building codes include various **anti-mob** upgrades. The mayor encouraged every family to add these upgrades to their homes.

Of course, since it's not yet required to do this, most families didn't bother . . . but if you recall how I had to walk Fluffles during the creeper scare, then you know my mom.

Besides, after hearing *anti-mob upgrades,* I envisioned **lava moats, piston traps**—you know, **crazy stuff** like that.

Yeah.
Right.

In reality, upgrading our house involved tearing up the wooden planks that served as the floor and replacing them with **cobblestone slabs.**

Then I had to dig up dirt in a five-block radius around the house and put **slabs** there.

"Slabs are resistant to **explosions,**" page seven of the building code manual states. "Slabs are heavy and annoying to properly place," *says twelve-year-old villager Runt.*

A house should have eaves so spiders can't climb onto the ceiling.

A fence should be made out of cobblestone to resist fire and explosions.

And then, building code A7F states that a door should be iron and **activated with a button** placed above, not a pressure plate, so that mobs can't open the door.

As if mobs **can't press buttons.**

That's how ridiculous the mayor is, you know?

Doesn't he understand how smart the **mobs** are?

The mobs are brilliant. Astoundingly, preposterously, ridiculously, improbably, absurdly, fantastically, wonderfully, unbelievably, amazingly, impossibly, **astonishingly brilliant.** If the mobs can come up with such tactics as zombie sandwiches, then surely they can press a button with a finger. And if they don't have fingers, then they'll just jump up and headbutt the buttons.

And if they don't have heads, well, I'm not sure *what* they'll do, but I'm willing to put one hundred emeralds on them figuring it out somehow.

There is one more thing **I didn't like** about all this additional iron and stone. After I performed all the necessary upgrades, our house looked . . . **colorless.** Emotionless. Devoid of warmth and feeling.

Gray walls.
Gray floors.
Gray fence.
Gray doors.

I'd include a picture of our new house, but **honestly,** it's extremely **depressing.** You'd probably start **crying.**

Even Steve commented on this. "If every house ends up like yours, this village will be straight out of a **dystopian film.**"

Dystopian?

I didn't know what that meant, but by the look on his face, I knew **it wasn't a good thing.**

Also . . . Pebble drew on my cloak with **red dye.**

I totally saw this coming.

After school, **Brio kidnapped** me again. As before, the **special building** was full of guys in **black robes.** And as before, Brio offered me a wide variety of snacks after we sat down in a small cobblestone room. In fact, he was **generally pleasant and happy,** until:

"By the way, Runt . . . have you seen **any slimes?**"

I began to sweat profusely.

"**Er,** once," I said. "The slime **incident.** If you remember."

"I mean **recently.**"

"**N-no,** of course not."

"Well, we've managed to re-create the potion you made earlier," he said. "It's called a **Rocket Potion.** Interestingly, the key ingredient—*that is, the extra ingredient used to augment a Potion of Leaping*—is **fermented glowstone.** This is made by combining regular glowstone with **a slimeball.**"

Of course. I can't remember how long it's been, but one day, I came home from school completely **exhausted.** The brewing teacher had given us some supplies—including glowstone—for us to do our homework with. But I was **so tired** I put the glowstone into **the wrong chest** in my bedroom. Perhaps my pet slime tried eating the glowstone, then spit it out?

As I thought about this, **awkward silence** filled the room. My mind raced as I considered what I could possibly say to **Brio**. Finally, I offered a **carefully** crafted response:

"Oh."

To be fair, it was a *bubbly* sounding "**oh.**" Naive. Innocent. *Full* of **innocence.** The most innocent "**oh**" that ever was. After hearing that "**oh,**" there should have been no doubt in anyone's mind that the only slime *I'd* seen in the past year was **the stuff** the school serves for **lunch** on Thursdays.

Brio removed his sunglasses. **Slowly.** Set them down upon the table in a **gentle** way. However, there was nothing gentle about his expression. Or the quiet tone of his voice:

"**We . . . are . . . at war** . . . if we are not careful, the mobs **will** destroy us . . . do **you . . . understand?**"

I held the sides of my seat. Arms locked straight. An effort to either hold myself upright or keep myself from **shaking** too much.

"Yes."

"**Good.** So, if you're **harboring** a mob . . . even something so innocent as, say, **a baby slime** . . . you will **report** it. **Immediately.**"

Wow. What a tough decision. What was he saying, anyway? **That Jello could be a spy?** No, I just **couldn't believe it.** Jello is a **nice slime.** A true gentleman, remember? In fact, someday, he's going to run for president. He wouldn't do a thing like that.

I didn't want to **betray** my village—but at the same time, I didn't want to turn in my pet, either. Besides, I felt my pet slime had a purpose . . . and it *wasn't* providing other mobs with **information.**

"Sir," I said, "I **do not have** any mobs in my possession."

Brio glanced down at the table, hands together, perhaps considering my words. When he spoke again, it was in his usual, **cheery tone:**

"**Very well. That's good news.** And there's *more* good news. Since you are directly responsible for the discovery of that potion recipe, you will be rewarded. Expect a payment of **fifty emeralds.** Within a few days."

More awkward silence, until:

"**Brio?** Can I ask what you were doing out there?"

"Out where?"

"**During the battle on Saturday.**"

"You are dismissed."

Brio rose up from his chair. I did the same.

"Oh, and look out for anything **strange,**" he said. "We have reason to believe there's **a spy** in the village."

"**A spy?**"

143

"Yes. You see, our data indicates the mobs wanted to destroy the school. How else could they have known where the school was located? Surely there must be a spy hiding somewhere within the periphery of the village. Or, possibly, **a traitor.** Understand?"

"Yes, sir."

I bowed before him and took off out of that place *(grabbing a few cookies as I did).*

As I ran back home, **my mind was racing.**

A spy in our village. **A traitor.**

Is it **Jello?** No, how can he spy on anything? All he does is eat bread. He never even leaves his box!

What about Breeze? She's **very weird,** after all.

Hurrrmm . . .

After I got back to my house, I went into my bedroom and opened the chest. Jello was there, sleeping. He woke up moments later and began **hopping around.**

I picked him up.

"You're not a spy, are you, Jello?"

I petted his flat head.

"No, of course not. **You're a good boy.**"

I've been mentioning my school for weeks but I've never shown it.
I suppose now would be a good time. After all, if the mobs really *do*
want to destroy it, then I should make a few pictures while I still can.

And so, say hello to the **Villager School of Minecraft
and Warriory.** *(Steve said warriory isn't an actual word. Yeah,
Steve, I get it: our vocabulary is different from yours on Earth.)*

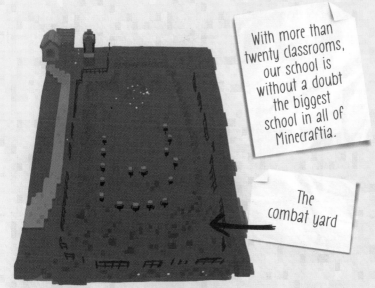

With more than twenty classrooms, our school is without a doubt the biggest school in all of Minecraftia.

The combat yard

By the way, an incident occurred in the combat yard today. Drill was
screaming at Max, so Max put a **sign** up on one of the dummies.

Ten minutes later, Drill came over, wondering why so many students
were attacking **the same dummy.**

Drill's Face

Anyone who attacked that sign had to do **two hundred laps.**
By the time we finished running, lunch was already over. Still, **the look
on Drill's face** when he saw that sign was priceless. I'd give up **ten
lunches** to see that again.

The front entrance

Obviously, the school hasn't seen the necessary **safety
upgrades** yet. Glass windows for walls probably aren't the safest way
to guard against zombies. **Just a guess, though.**

The cafeteria

You're probably wondering how **150 students** manage to sit down in this place. They don't. The food here makes mushroom stew look tasty.

And this is why I always
bring <u>my own</u> lunch.

See that **green potato?** That's a **fermented** potato. It's a village specialty. Made using **a secret crafting recipe.** Most adults consider it **a delicacy,** and it's supposed to be healthy. That's why it's on the menu, I guess.

By the way, I wasn't joking about **the slime** they serve on Thursdays. It's that bowl of **green stew** on the right. It isn't really slime, of course, although it looks just like it. **Grass stew.** Another villager **"delicacy."** My grandfather loves the stuff.

Okay, I'm just gonna rush through the rest of the tour because it's **not very interesting,** and honestly, I'm getting a bit hungry.

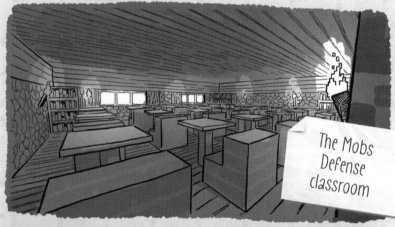

The Mobs Defense classroom

Crafting classroom

The Tower

I've never been to the second and third floors.
I think the teachers do **weird experiments** up there.

Brewing
classroom

149

Near the school is the village square. It's a trading zone, full of merchant stands.

The fountain. The mayor ordered **its construction** years ago. After it was built, that old blacksmith, Leaf, took off his shoes and began **washing his feet.** Many people have **avoided its waters** since.

The square's food stand. My **favorite stand. Obviously.** If I had saved up all my emeralds instead of buying junk food at this place, I'd probably have enough for **a full set of diamond armor** by now. Kids who forgot to bring their own lunch and can't stomach grass stew go here.

The stand that shall not be mentioned—although I will say the roof, made out of acacia and birch to resemble a giant red mushroom, is **kinda neat.**

That was a **ton** of pictures. Sorry. Wait, what am I apologizing for?! **It took me forever to draw those pictures!**

Anyway, there you have it. To be honest, that was only about *half* the places I could have shown you, but I didn't want you **to fall asleep.**

Oh. I received that payment from Brio. So I went **shopping** today and ended up buying a **full set of leather armor** *(except for a helmet)* along with **an iron sword** and **two enchanted books.**

Then . . . In the street just outside the blacksmith . . . I ran into **Pebble.** He eyed me, eyed my sword, then **smirked** and stepped closer.

"I see you've brought me **a gift.**"

"Don't even try it," I said, raising the blade for the first time. "This thing's enchanted with **Bane of Noobs V** and **Wuss Slaying VII.**"

151

NOOBSLAYER
COMBAT
SHARPNESS I
BLOCKING II
+ 8.25 ATTACK DAMAGE

He put his hands in the air and backed up slowly.

"Oh, dear! No! Please!" He dropped to one knee and clasped his hands together. "Please spare a humble noob such as myself!" Two of his friends came around the corner then, glanced at us, and snickered. Then the three of them took off.

Sigh. I'd been trying to avoid him, but I guess that's impossible now. At least he didn't dunk me in the well again. I should be thankful for that. He did that yesterday, but I didn't put it into my diary. It was just too humiliating. I wish there was a Bane of Noobs enchantment, though.

Pebble would have been totally
shaking in his boots.

THURSDAY

This morning, **Brio and company** showed up at school. They set up **an office** on the second floor. And the whole day, they observed everyone. They also randomly searched **through kids' inventories** in the hallways and dug through our school chests . . .

It was eerie. You couldn't go anywhere without being **watched,** without being searched, followed, or endlessly questioned.

Then, during Intro to Combat, a few of those black-robed guys stepped in. They made us run in place for a **long time** and shouted in our faces while we did it. A guy in black was yelling at Stump so loud that spit was flying from his mouth. **Poor Stump** was moving as fast as he could, arms swinging, knees moving up and down like pistons, with the most **scared yet serious** look upon his face.

*(I refer to them as "guys in black" because I really don't know who they are. They're **elders,** certainly, but I don't know any of their names. The only thing I do know about them is that they're not **complete noobs** like Urf.)*

Annoyingly, Pebble and Emerald seemed immune to their **harassment.** Neither of them have received a question, an inventory search, or even an angry look.

I want out.

Lightning, please **strike me** and turn me into a **witch**.

Or an enderpumpkin.
Or a **creeperman**.

I don't even know what a **creeperman** is or what a creeperman's life would be like, but **I don't care.** I'll take it. Anything is better than this.

If my life hit **bedrock** yesterday, then today, it somehow broke through that **bedrock** and vanished deep down into the **void**.

Today, they assigned every student to a **"combat unit."** Should the mobs **attack again**, we must stay with the other members of our **unit** and follow Drill's orders. Sounds good, **right? Yeah.** Here are the other three members of my unit:

It's almost like the mayor spent a whole night **calculating** how to **annoy me the most.**

Emerald didn't seem **too happy** about it, either.

"You can't do this," she said to Drill.

When the teacher chuckled but said nothing, she **continued:**

"**Hey!** I *refuse* to group up with them. **Especially him.** The **weirdest stuff** always happens to him! He's like a lightning rod for trouble! **A magnet for craziness!**"

She was referring to me, obviously. *(Do I really get into that much trouble? It's not like I ever asked for it. Stuff happens, you know?)* Besides, I didn't do anything crazy during **the battle on Saturday.** I stuck with my friends. **Protected** them. Even resisted the urge to **follow Brio.** Emerald's **silvery voice** tore me from my thoughts.

"**How about that creepy girl?** What are you *thinking* putting the two of them together? And don't get me started on Urf. He's totally—"

She fell silent when Brio walked up.

"**There is a reason for everything,**" he said. "Trust me."

The "**war heroine**" lowered her head, fists clenched—but she waited for Brio to take off before letting out **a big sigh.**

Hurrrmm.
This is gonna be fun.

I'm stuck with **Weirdostalkergirl, The Great Bearded Noob,** and **Princess Hissyfit McCrybaby.** Good thing I like **a challenge,** eh? Stump arguably has it **worse,** however. He's grouped with Bumbi, who is currently the lowest-level student in the whole school. Apparently, he still has a **combat score of 1.** How is that even possible? A door has more than that.

Anyway, **I'll be okay.** Tomorrow, there's no school and no chance of another attack. I mean, the mobs attacked *last* Saturday, **right?** The mobs would *never* attack on *another* Saturday because that would be too predictable. **Yeah.** I'm totally safe. Tomorrow, I'm going fishing. And I'm getting some ice cream. And I'm hanging out with my friends.

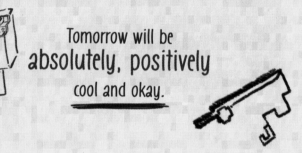

Tomorrow will be
absolutely, positively
cool and okay.

"YOU'RE FACING THE WRONG WAY YOU SU——"

BOOM!!!

An **explosion** drowned out whatever insult Drill was about to **hurl**. Beyond him, the streets might have passed for one of the nicer parts of **the Nether.**

As Emerald said when we first arrived,

"You know, this would make a good ad for promoting those village building codes."

Fires were **blazing**, the ground was occasionally trembling, and **the smoke,** drifting across the ground on its little gray feet, made it impossible to see just how many mobs there were out there. A lot, I guessed.

"FIRE!!"

Arrows flew from **rooftops** in endless streams, vanishing into the gray mist. Earlier, we'd cut down almost every tree in the park to make a countless number of shafts. Those who were the best shots with a bow had been put into the same unit. Minutes ago, they'd been sent to the tops of houses. **It was nice having archers.**

Our unit was assigned to the ground to fight the **enemy with swords**, and with **so many arrows** flying, we didn't have to do that much. The sheer number of arrows the archers sent out caught the mobs by surprise. Some sections of wall could barely be seen due to the amount of arrows sticking in them.

It was intense.

Then, like the last battle, the mobs started **to run**. **Ridiculously,** a zombie broke out into a really funny dance before it took off.

"GET!! THAT!! ZOMBIE!!"

At Drill's command, over one hundred screaming villagers charged forward . . . along with Steve, Mike, and my two best friends. At last, the archers **jumped down** and followed at a safe distance.

But my unit wouldn't be joining them. We were on **guard duty.** Our job was to protect the school, just in case the mobs pulled **any tricks.**

We had to prevent **any creeper** from getting within five blocks. Drill turned to us. Surprisingly, he didn't shout or even raise his voice:

"**Remain near the school** until further notice."

I nodded. Then Breeze nodded. Then Emerald nodded. But Urf was nowhere nearby. He was walking down the road, **trying to sneak away.**

"And where might *you* be going?" Drill called out.

The elder slowly turned around.

"Well, **uh,** you know, I just thought I might, um, go check on something—"

The current combat teacher smiled, beckoning him closer with a finger.

Urf finally nodded—*but glumly, glumly. Then he trudged back into the blazing street.*

"**Now,**" said Drill, "if you guys get into any trouble, just set these off." He handed Emerald some **blue fireworks** along with a flint and steel. "And don't leave the school." With that, he sprinted off through the smoke, which was only swirling at knee level now. The four of us silently watched him go.

In the distance, an occasional explosion or shout could be heard.

We were alone.

I wanted to **be out there**, of course, **next to my friends**, but we had to obey our orders.

160

There were no mobs here, and it seemed like there never would be, but maybe Drill **was right.**

I sighed and glanced behind me,
at the school.
The sounds of combat faded. And then—

SATURDAY: BOSS BATTLE—PART TWO

To the right, distant footsteps could be heard.
It was more like scraping, shuffling.

Zombies.

"I heard that!" Urf jerked his head every which way. There was another scraping sound. Then the elder made the same **ridiculous creeper** face, the same pigman grunt.

"Mobs! **They're around the corner!** I heard them!"

"Will you *shut up*," I hissed.

The school was across the square, which meant that if we ran there now, the mobs would **surely see us.** So I motioned for everyone to hide. All four of us crept into the alley to the right. Urf latched on to Emerald, **trembling.**

"Don't let them get me!"

"Go away!" She pushed him back and glared at him. "Dude, you're such a—"

Just then, **several zombies** walked into view and stopped in front of the fountain. Their **deep, guttural** voices drifted through the air. They were speaking in the **ancient tongue.**

It took me a moment to realize **what one of them was holding.**

"You forgot zombie demolitions expert. Punk."

Emerald drew her sword.

"I call dibs on **Explody** there."

"He's mine."

With a loud scream, I charged, sword held in both hands. I don't know why I was being so reckless. Just . . . when I saw that zombie holding a block of TNT, **something snapped inside of me.**

I mean, who did they think they were? **They were zombies.**

They were supposed to **moan.** Burn in the sun.

Get **confused** by improperly set doors.

My sword sliced through the air. However . . . after connecting with its target, it was as if the blade had **struck cobblestone** instead of rotten flesh. **The zombie didn't moan,** stumble back, or even flinch—instead, it punched me so hard I flew five blocks backward and landed on my back. Despite my armor, the attack reduced my life **by four hearts.** That was a **huge amount of damage** from a single attack. Yet it couldn't match the amount of pain I felt.

Ten blocks to my right, Emerald had **skidded** to a halt and was now slowly backpedaling into the ruined street. Urf, of course, had already fled the scene. I thought I was a **goner.** Then **Breeze** yanked me to my feet.

Silly girl . . . What is she doing?

We just **stood** there, while more zombies trickled in from **every direction**.

Within moments, at least ten had surrounded us.

We were cut off. We couldn't run.

Yet . . . they didn't close in. Instead, several of them laughed, chests heaving, heads raised back, faces somehow **jovial.** Their deep laughter echoed across the square.

That was when I noticed the **swirls emanating from their bodies.**

Red swirls.

That meant the zombies were under the effect of **strength potions**—maybe **Strength III,** considering how much damage I had taken from one punch. There were **faint gray swirls,** too, although I had no idea what kind of effect they signified.

After another round of **laughter,** the zombies moved in, one step at a time, **impossibly slow,** as if they were trying to draw this moment out and **prolong our suffering.**

Then a zombie began speaking, its voice screechy yet deep. It was gibberish, **unintelligible,** the language of **enchanting tables and wizards** long since forgotten. Still, even though I couldn't understand the words, I knew what was being said: **We were doomed.** There was no way out of this.

There was just no way.

Then, behind me, ringing out above the zombie's frightening speech, was **a metallic cling.**

Breeze.

It was the first time she'd drawn her sword in battle. When I glanced behind me, I noticed she **wasn't trembling** like before. On the contrary—she stood **perfectly still.** It was as if she had suddenly **grown stronger** while I had **grown weak.**

I found her courage **inspiring,** yet it ultimately wouldn't matter. The zombies were **impossibly strong, impossibly resilient.**

She's fighting even though there's **no way we can win.**

And **I ignored** her this whole time . . .

"Run," I said. "I'll distract them, huh? **Just run."**

SATURDAY: BOSS BATTLE—PART THREE

I . . . don't know what happened. There's . . . really **no way to explain it.** In less than ten seconds, **piles of dust were scattered everywhere** . . . I stood there for a long time, my mind a malfunctioning **redstone machine.** A light breeze scattered the dust.

Breeze was staring at the ground, her expression **dark.**

"You can't tell anyone."

"So . . . you've been **hiding yourself?**"

No response.

She turned away.

I studied her for a moment—then, after realizing she wasn't going **to talk anymore,** I surveyed the destruction in her wake. **Tons of items** lay within the zombie's remains. Armor, swords. Bows. Arrows. Flint and steel. Tools of all kinds and **a great deal of potions.** Even a **bone.** Those zombies were really packing. Especially the zombie Emerald had dubbed **"Explody."** TNT had **spilled out everywhere** after Breeze took him out. Had we not been sent here on guard duty, the school would be **ten times worse** than that street over there.

Good job, Drill. When this is all over, I'm gonna buy you a pie.

I picked up all the items, wondering **how many emeralds** I could get for all of it.

Speaking of emeralds, Emerald eventually came back with two iron golems. Not a bad idea. She met the **square** with wide eyes.

"What *happened?*"

"It's **complicated.**"

Then, the ground trembled. Again, **deep laughter** boomed in the distance—**but this time, it wasn't from any zombie.**

To the south, down another ruined street, perhaps a little more than **fifty blocks** away, stood the **legend** himself: **Urkk Doomwhip.**

Two creepers slithered around at his feet, like baby chickens in comparison. *(Important note: One of them was glowing a brilliant shade of blue.)*

Needless to say, Emerald did more **backpedaling.**

"WoW," she said. "They **really, really** want the school. I say we **compromise.** We could let them take out the combat yard. Then we'd all shake hands and call it a day. I mean, they'd be **doing us a favor anyway,** y'know?"

The two iron golems charged. Breeze sagged her shoulders and followed them in. Emerald and I ran after her.

"Wait!" I called out. "He's gonna—"

And yes. It can really do this.

Yeah. He's gonna do that.

Even though I'd already read about Urkk's ability to **throw other mobs,** it still came as a shock, seeing that **creeper** fly, its sad little face growing bigger and bigger . . .

We had to **take cover. Snark's Tavern** was the closest place.

There used to be a sign here that said something about Steve owing Snark sixty-seven emeralds. I guess he lost a bet during an **iron golem race.**

We **burst through** the door.

What a cozy little place. Stump and I often went to Snark's when we were kids. The tea is pretty good. **Sadly,** there was no time for tea now. On the plus side, **we were safe.**

Snark said his tavern is the only original building still standing after the **creeper rush of 1511.** Little did I know, Breeze, Emerald, and I were nothing more than the **Three Little Pigs,** with the incoming charged creeper as the Big Bad Wolf.

And Snark's Tavern?
Just so much straw.

I guess Snark **failed to mention** that the only other homes around in 1511 were made of dirt and/or grass.

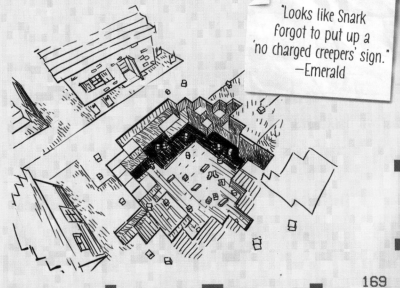

"Looks like Snark forgot to put up a 'no charged creepers' sign."
—Emerald

169

When the smoke cleared, I spotted **several iron ingots** down in the crater. The remains of the iron golems. They must have taken a direct hit. **Poor things.**

(There was also some leather armor, which I can only guess was from a zombie that tried running after us.)

After **glancing** at the crater, Breeze **left the building** without a word. She ran so fast I couldn't keep up. Then she jumped— *a height of five blocks, impossible—*and struck Urkk square in the face. From what I'd read, Urkk had an **incredible amount of life,** yet her attack not only **forced him back,** but **shattered** his **black helmet as well.**

However . . . When she landed, the pigman sent out his **chained hook.** I only had time to see Urkk's hook **snag Breeze** and pull her within arm's reach . . . Then he smashed her with one of his **huge, block-sized fists,** like an iron golem hitting a baby rabbit. Breeze went flying. Somewhere over a house. **She vanished beyond the roof.**

She's okay, I thought. For all I know, she **probably has more life than Urkk does.**

Emerald glanced at the **smoldering crater,** at the melted remains of the iron golems, at the sky where Breeze had flown, and at the **enormous** zombie pigman with glowing **red eyes** and a crazy-looking fishing rod who'd just thrown a creeper roughly **twenty-five blocks.**

170

There was a brief silence as she reflected upon the situation, then: *"That's it.* **I'm outta here.***"*

After she took off, I did some glancing around, too. A little glance here, a little glance there. Real innocent. Casual. **Unfortunately,** Urkk was glancing, too. At me.

Hurrrmm . . .
This is baddd.

SATURDAY: BOSS BATTLE—PART FIVE

For a second, I actually **took out my shovel.**

Okay, think. What did Max say about Urkk's fear of **heights?** Something about a height of **five blocks?** But it's all stone down here.

Just my luck! I have no time to **dig a pit** wide and deep enough to scare him. I'd need **an enchanted diamond pickaxe.**

(I guess your plans can't all be brilliant, eh, Max?)

Okay.
Run for now.

I **climbed** out of the hole and took off to the square.

Urkk ran, too—and let me tell you, I'd never really thought about just **how fast a giant pigman can run,** but believe me, it's fast.

171

He had **nearly** caught up to me by the time I reached the square. I looked behind me, saw him **sending out his chain** . . .

. . . **and dashed** to the right just before it caught me.

The chain made a **high-pitched whine** as it cut through the air inches from my left ear. **Urkk roared.** His voice was so loud and deep.

"You quick one! Like **big rabbit!** Me love rabbit stew! Hur, hur, hur."

I couldn't **run** from him, so I had to hide.

If I can hide, and **survive** long enough, maybe someone will come over and **help me out.**

Actually, on that note, **where is everyone else?!** Preoccupied, I guess. There are still more iron golems, though.

Step 1: Dig a hole.

Step 2: Hide from Urkk.

Step 3: Wait until iron golems save me.

Impressed? Neither am I. **Neither am I.** But it was all I had. Yet . . . if I tried digging out in the open, the pigman would hook me, and that would be that.

I had to find cover. The closest thing was . . . **the mushroom stew stand.** Today was definitely *not* my day. It had a **low roof,** though, so I knew it would be hard for Urkk to see me. The huge pigman sent out his hook, and I dodged again. Then I dove into the stand.

A **brown mushroom** was growing on the grass floor. Still holding my shovel, I dug **down into the grass.**

From there, I could only see Urkk's legs. The **ground shook** as the pigman took a step forward.

Then the second creeper caught up to him,
and Urkk grabbed it . . .

A second later, **I heard a thud.** Above me. **And a hiss.** Yes, Urkk had tossed the creeper onto the roof of the mushroom stew stand.

(Can these mobs get any more annoying?)

The scientific and technical term used to describe the roof would be *splinters.* **Splinters everywhere.** The smoke cleared, exposing Urkk's huge face, **staring down at me.** He raised his huge fist back to send out his chained hook.

It was over. He was going to eat me. *At least Max and Stump aren't here to see this,* I thought. *I hope **Breeze is okay** . . .*

Then something **amazing** happened . . .

 Jello appeared.

He bounced over the counter of the mushroom stand and **hopped up** and down in front of me. The giant pigman **scowled and shook with rage.**

"Move!!"

Jello hopped again and made some **weird noises.**

He's . . . protecting me?!

"I said **scram,** slime!! **This one's mine!!**"

More hopping. More squeaking. **Well,** it was nice that my pet slime had come to my rescue, but even *I* knew there was nothing Jello could do except buy me some time.

Then the following words echoed in my mind:

"... *height* of five blocks ..."

An idea began forming. There was a way to defeat Urkk. It was **complicated,** I realized, but maybe . . .

I looked at the oak planks scattered around me. At the brown mushroom growing on the ground. Then I glanced at the bone, the flint and steel, and the TNT in my inventory. **Yes,** piece by piece, I was formulating a **ridiculous plan** . . . I had no idea if it would work, honestly.

"Distract him, Jello! Okay?!"

"Squerk!" *(Maybe that's how slimes say "okay"?)*

With shaking hands, I grabbed four oak planks and crafted a crafting table. Urkk kept yelling at my pet.

"Just a few more seconds, Jello!"

Squerk!! Squerk!!

Finally, I turned the bone into a few **handfuls of bone meal.** Of course, the whole time, Urkk was shouting.

"So you've sided with them?! **Traitor!!** Time to join your friend!!"

The pigman raised his weapon again.

"Jello!! Run!!"

I pushed the baby slime out of the way, then dove backward over the counter, away from Urkk.

There was a **crackling** sound as the hook drove into the oak wood between us. Another roar, followed by **his footsteps.**

Boom, boom.

He was standing on top of the mushroom stand's front counter, now. He looked down at me, his face visible again, and **licked his lips** . . .

I ran away, knowing that hook would be coming for me. It cut through the air. **A horrifying sound**. Yet I turned around and let it hook me. . .

* * *

Ooof. Urkk pulled that chain with all his **might.** Even though it was just a special type of fishing rod, it dealt a huge amount of damage when it reeled me in. Still, I grasped the end and unhooked myself before his massive fist grabbed me.

I **dropped** to the ground, taking slight falling damage. But the brown mushroom now sat before me. More important, the mushroom sat **under Urkk's legs.** As Urkk raised a foot to stomp me into villager stew, another arrow whistled through the air, **striking** Urkk in the face.

Breeze?
She's alive!

The arrow didn't do much to the pigman, but he put his foot down and looked up for a second. **Another distraction.** It bought just enough time for me to dump a handful of bone meal onto the mushroom. Green motes of light flew forth . . . and the mushroom **instantly** grew . . . . . . pushing Urkk up high into the air.

Uwaaaaahhhhh!!!

It was amazing.

The giant brown mushroom **not only forced Urkk upward**, but also somehow supported his weight. Up that high, with Urkk's fear of heights, he must have felt like a skeleton surrounded by fifty dogs, or an enderman on a tiny island in the middle of the ocean . . .

You get the idea.

"You will pay for this!! **Herobrine** is coming!!"

I **ignored** his cries, grabbing all the **TNT** from my inventory. There was only one thing left to do.

Once I lit a TNT block, I grabbed Jello and ran. I guess Urkk was too scared to even try to do anything to me. He just cowered up there on top of the giant mushroom, as I sprinted to safety.

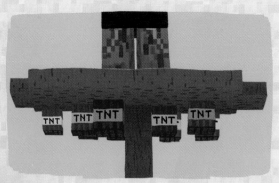

"You . . . little . . . runt!! Uwaaaag!!"

Cloudy, with a chance of mushroom-and-pigman stew . . .

A slight wind rustled the grass nearby. **Experience orbs** flowed through the sky. The wind calmed down. Urkk's fishing rod had landed **five blocks away**. I **petted** Jello, wondering how he'd gotten out of his chest.

"Good boy."

Squeak.

Only then did I **feel the pain.** My vision kept flashing bright red, and my life bar was flickering the same color. **I had half a heart left.** I slid down against the wall, **my vision growing blurry,** dim.

Within moments,
everything went black.

Don't worry. **Everything's okay.**

I didn't get much recognition for **dropping Urkk**, since Breeze was the only one to witness it, but hey, how can I complain? **I'm alive.**

By the way, one of the first things I did after waking up was ask Breeze if I could see her record book. **She actually showed me.**

BREEZE
STUDENT
LEVEL 98

MINING	97%
COMBAT	100%
TRADING	91%
FARMING	100%
BUILDING	100%
CRAFTING	100%

Turns out **everyone at school was wrong**. Breeze has been **rank one** almost the entire time. Which means Pebble is rank two, Emerald rank three, and so on. Whoever was rank three a couple of weeks ago is **still a mystery**.

My own level is getting up there.

RUNT
STUDENT
LEVEL 81

MINING	57%
COMBAT	89%
TRADING	100%
FARMING	79%
BUILDING	95%
CRAFTING	68%

I'm **currently rank five**. Breeze, Pebble, Emerald, and Max are ahead of me. If I slip up, maybe **I won't become a warrior after all**. But at this rate, the mayor's gonna have to let everyone become warriors, so maybe it doesn't matter. No. It will matter. I'm sure of it.

Breeze and I went to get ice cream this afternoon, and she told me more about herself.

"When I saw **everyone competing** and showing off," Breeze said, "I knew I shouldn't try to draw attention to myself. That way, I wouldn't receive any **harassment** from someone like Pebble."

"Why didn't I think of that?" I paused. "Wait a second. Remember the archery range? Your shooting wasn't too great then."

"I wasn't actually trying," she said. "After the first five shots, you noticed, so I . . ."

Right. Anyway, I think there's even more to this weird girl than she's letting on—she's obviously not ordinary—but **she won't tell me anything** about her family, where she comes from, or anything like that.

"I've been following you because my dad asked me to," she said. "My dad has been **watching you.** He thinks the village needs you."

"Needs me? **Why?**"

She gazed at the endless blue sky, **lost in thought.**

"Maybe you're not the best student, but my dad thinks you have **great potential.**"

"**Really . . .?**"

(I think this was the first compliment I've ever received in my life.)

". . . and who's your dad?" I asked.

. . .

"Well?"

"You'll find out **soon enough.**"

Hurrgg.

I really wonder who her father is . . . Someone told me he was some **wealthy miner** type or something like that, but who knows.

I also found out *she* had let Jello out. After Urkk knocked her away, she ran to my house and grabbed him. She thought that maybe he could talk to the pigman, since he's a **mob** and all. It was worth a shot and bought me enough time to **blow up the pigman.**

Of course, I was wondering **how she knew about Jello,** since I'd never told her about him.

"It was Stump, **wasn't it?!**"

"No, no. Um, I . . . saw you **playing with him once.** Through your bedroom window."

As for the village, things are **getting grim**. This second mob attack has sent the **mayor into a panic** and prompted him to rigidly enforce the building codes, among other things. The village is becoming more and more **gray** . . . stone and iron everywhere . . .

And the guys in black robes harass us in school every day.

"Study **harder!** Run **faster!** What do you think the mobs are doing?! They're training sixteen hours a day!"

"Spies and traitors will be **imprisoned without question**."

If you have reason to believe someone you know is providing the mobs with information, please **contact** . . ."

"We are **searching your inventories** and school chests for the **safety** of the village . . ."

"Anyone who goes outside after sunset will be **detained for questioning** . . ."

The last thing I have to add is . . . a lot of **huge building projects** are underway. Deadfall fields are to be dug outside—a huge project, considering how big the wall is. Then guards will be placed on the walls at night. In addition, a new tower will be built, **an extremely tall one,** to detect incoming attacks.

From here on out, we can't have **any more mobs breaking any more walls.** The crazier the mobs get, the crazier our defenses will get. **It's that simple.**

Herobrine can eat
a fermented potato.

YOU KNOW
the drill by now.

I had to stop somewhere!
The story picks right up in book 3:

Cube Kid is the pen name of Erik Gunnar Taylor, a writer who has lived in Alaska his whole life. A big fan of video games—especially Minecraft—he discovered early that he also had a passion for writing fan fiction.

Cube Kid's unofficial Minecraft fan fiction series, *Diary of a Wimpy Villager*, came out as e-books in 2015 and immediately met with great success in the Minecraft community. They were published in France by 404 éditions in paperback with illustrations by Saboten and now return in this same format to Cube Kid's native country under the title *Diary of an 8-Bit Warrior*.

When not writing, Cube Kid likes to travel, putter with his car, devour fan fiction, and play his favorite video game.